"I usually don't spend the night with a man I just met. You were the first and the last."

"I'm honored that you picked me. I enjoyed our time together."

Her warm eyes flashed that Lana had, too. She had a mouth made for loving. Plump, soft lips that were naturally pink. They parted a fraction, just as they had seconds before he'd kissed her the other night.

Sly definitely wanted t̶̶̶̶̶̶ her and explore t̶̶̶̶̶̶̶̶̶̶̶̶̶̶̶̶ assion and enj̶̶̶̶̶̶̶̶̶̶̶̶̶̶̶̶̶̶̶̶ night togethe̶̶̶̶̶̶̶̶̶̶̶̶̶̶̶̶̶ her hair behind ̶̶̶̶̶̶̶̶̶̶̶̶̶̶̶̶.

He want̶̶̶̶̶̶̶̶̶̶̶̶̶̶̶̶̶ too much.

The strength of his need scared him. If he was smart, he'd turn around and leave. But his legs refused to budge.

Dear Reader,

This is the first book in my Prosperity, Montana miniseries. Prosperity is a fictitious town in north central Montana—gorgeous country. With ranches, great places to hike, wonderful restaurants and stunning Prosperity Falls, the waterfall that draws tourists and locals, what's not to love? I had fun creating the town and look forward to further developing it as I write new stories.

Sly Pettit, a successful rancher, hasn't had life easy. The oldest of three siblings (don't worry, they'll get their own books), Sly had to grow up fast. Except for his little sister, he doesn't trust anyone. He likes living alone.

Lana Carpenter owns a day care. Almost six years ago, Lana married and settled into what she thought was her happily ever after. Her dream ended when her husband left her for someone else. Lana longs for a family of her own.

I loved writing Sly and Lana's story, and hope you'll enjoy reading about them.

Enjoy!

Ann

P.S. I always appreciate hearing from readers. Email me at ann@annroth.net, write me c/o P.O. Box 25003, Seattle, WA 98165-1903, or visit my Facebook page. And please visit my website, at www.annroth.net, where you can sign up for my newsletter and enter the monthly drawing to win a free, autographed book! Be sure to visit the Fun Stuff page, where you'll find my blog, recipes and other fun stuff.

For even more, check out my Ann Roth Author page on Facebook and follow me on Twitter: @Ann_Roth.

A RANCHER'S HONOR

—

ANN ROTH

HARLEQUIN® AMERICAN ROMANCE®

ISBN-13: 978-0-373-75525-7

A RANCHER'S HONOR

Printed in U.S.A.

ABOUT THE AUTHOR

Ann Roth lives in the greater Seattle area with her husband. After earning an MBA she worked as a banker and corporate trainer. She gave up the corporate life to write, and if they awarded PhDs in writing happily-ever-after stories, she'd surely have one.

Ann loves to hear from readers. You can write her at P.O. Box 25003, Seattle, WA 98165-1903, or email her at ann@annroth.net.

Books by Ann Roth

HARLEQUIN AMERICAN ROMANCE

1031—THE LAST TIME WE KISSED
1103—THE BABY INHERITANCE
1120—THE MAN SHE'LL MARRY
1159—IT HAPPENED ONE WEDDING
1174—MITCH TAKES A WIFE
1188—ALL I WANT FOR CHRISTMAS
1204—THE PILOT'S WOMAN
1252—OOH, BABY!
1266—A FATHER FOR JESSE
1390—RANCHER DADDY*
1408—MONTANA DOCTOR*
1436—HER RANCHER HERO*
1456—THE RANCHER SHE LOVED*
1472—A RANCHER'S CHRISTMAS*

*Saddlers Prairie

To my wonderful readers. You're the best!

Chapter One

Lana Carpenter woke up with the worst headache ever. With a groan, she cracked one eye open to glance at the clock on the bedside table. But there was no clock, and the dark wood table was nothing like her oak furniture.

She wasn't in her queen-size bed at her town house— she was in a king-size bed in a hotel room, and judging by the monogram on the sheets, it was the Prosperity Inn, one of Prosperity, Montana's, four-star hotels.

Both eyes were open now. After stealing a peek at the other side of the bed—it was empty, but a dented pillow lay close to hers—she sat up quickly, grimacing at the sudden thundering in her temples.

The clock on that side of the bed said it was just after ten. She never slept this late—even if it was Saturday!

She pulled the dented pillow to her face and the lingering scent of a man's spicy aftershave tickled her nostrils. One whiff and everything flooded back.

Kate picking her up and commiserating with her over the fact that Brent and Julia had had their baby. Driving to the Bitter & Sweet Bar and Grill for dinner and dancing to a live country-and-western band. Consuming too little dinner and too many cocktails in an effort to forget her ex's betrayal. The handsome cowboy at the table across the way, and the strong attraction that had flared between them from the first moment of eye contact.

On the way to the bar, Lana hadn't even thought about meeting a man. She was still recovering from the divorce and had only wanted to forget that Brent's new wife had given him the one thing Lana couldn't—a baby.

Then the sexy cowboy had asked her to dance, and they'd kept on dancing, with short stops for drinks and casual chitchat in between. After a while Kate had grown bored and left. Lana had stayed, with the intention of finding a cab later to take her home. But she'd soon forgotten all about the cab when dancing progressed to long, passionate kisses and the haste to rent a room within walking distance so that she and the cowboy could...

"Oh, dear God, I didn't!" she muttered, shattering the quiet.

Her clothes lay in a telltale trail that started just inside the door and ended near the bed.

She definitely had.

Which was so unlike her. Another groan escaped from her. Normally, she wasn't much of a drinker. Oh, sure, she enjoyed an occasional glass of wine with dinner, but that was pretty much it. She'd never picked up a stranger, either.

Sly, that was his name, had assured her that he was clean—Lana recalled that. She'd stated that she was clean and healthy, too. Shortly after Brent had left her for Julia some eighteen months ago, she'd had herself tested. She hadn't been with a man since.

Until last night.

She and Sly had more than made up for her year and a half of celibacy. Boy, had they.

Her cheeks warmed. Then she remembered that sometime during the night, as they lay tangled together after making love, he'd explained he'd have to leave for work early in the morning. Lana was glad he'd let her sleep instead of waking her to say goodbye, because facing him this morning would have been, at best, uncomfortable.

Mother Nature called. Clutching her head, Lana made her way to the bathroom. There on the counter she found a bottle of aspirin and an unopened half liter of water. Under the water, a note.

Last night was great. This should help with the hangover.

Bless the man for his thoughtfulness. After swallowing several pain tablets with a healthy quantity of water, she studied herself in the mirror. Despite her headache, she looked radiant, as if she was still basking in the afterglow of a night of unbridled passion. Sly was right—last night had been great.

A long shower helped revive her, and by the time she dried off, fixed her hair and dressed in last night's clothes—clean clothes would have been nice, but Lana didn't have any with her—she felt almost normal.

She was shrugging into her coat to leave when her cell phone chirped "It's Raining Men." Kate's favorite song. Lana picked up right away. "Hey there."

"You were supposed to call this morning with the scoop. Tell me that handsome cowboy you were dancing with gave you a ride home."

Lana glanced at the unmade bed, winced and plopped onto a chair. "Not exactly."

"You're saying you turned him down and took a cab instead? That's a crying shame, Lana, because for the first time in forever, you were actually having fun with a really hot guy."

Kate was right about the hot part. Tall, lean and muscled,

with startling silvery-blue eyes and a killer smile, Sly was every woman's cowboy fantasy. Lana caught herself in a dreamy sigh and frowned. "He never offered me a ride."

"Well, shoot. And he seemed so into you. How much longer did you dance before you parted company?"

"Um…actually, we didn't part company. I'm at the Prosperity Inn." Which was only a few short blocks from the Bitter & Sweet.

"What are you doing at a hotel?" Kate asked, then answered her own question with a singsong "Oh." Her voice softened to an excited whisper. "You should have said something sooner. Call me later."

"It's okay—he's not here."

"You mean he's in the shower?"

"No, I mean he had to leave early this morning to go to work. I slept in."

"It's not like you to spend the night with a guy you just met."

"Tell me about it." As a rule, Lana waited for that level of intimacy until she was in a relationship. "I can't believe I did this."

"Hey, it happens. Did you at least enjoy yourself?"

Lana didn't have to think long about that. Now that her headache was all but gone, other things bubbled into her mind. Good memories that made her whole body hum. "It was pretty special."

"Ooh. Gonna share some details?"

"No!"

"At least give me his name? Maybe what he does for a living?"

"His name is Sly and I assume he's a rancher. He must be, right? Who else has to get up at the crack of dawn to go to work on a Saturday? I don't know his last name or anything else about him, except that he's never been married. I said I was divorced."

In the heat of the moment, she'd also mentioned that she couldn't have kids. "We agreed that this was a night to forget our troubles and keep things fun and light." They'd accomplished both goals, in spades. "I don't think we'll ever see each other again."

"That's so unlike you."

"So you said." As unforgettable as last night had been, Lana regretted what she'd done. She massaged the space between her eyes. "Remind me to never drink again."

"Don't be so hard on yourself. Look on the positive side—you're back in the saddle, and a darned handsome cowboy put you there." Kate hooted at her joke. "Besides, you needed to be wild for one night. Once you adopt a baby, you won't be able to overdo the alcohol or stay out all night on a whim."

"I never do either of those things."

"You did last night. Listen, I have to leave for my mani-pedi, but if you need a ride, I can come pick you up in an hour or so."

Lana supposed she could order breakfast downstairs and wait, but she wanted to change into fresh clothes. She also had a jillion things to do today—clean her house, grocery shop, do laundry, et cetera. "I'll take a cab, thanks. Send me a picture of your nails."

"Will do. Talk to you later."

Early April in western Montana usually brought mornings cold enough to see your own breath. Yet this morning, Sly Pettit was sweating like a son of a dog. He also felt like crap. At thirty-five he was no longer able to shake off a hangover with a couple of aspirin as easily as he'd done at thirty.

"Sly? I said, if you're feelin' poorly, Ollie, Bean and I can handle the rest of the branding."

Ace, Sly's longtime foreman, was staring at him oddly, and Bean, a grizzled cowhand, wore a frown. Ollie, a rangy twenty-year-old kid Sly had hired for the spring and summer, shot him a curious glance.

Sly realized he was grimacing and smoothed his expression. When he'd met his attorney at the Bitter & Sweet Bar and Grill for dinner last night, he'd planned on staying about an hour, then heading home. Instead, he'd arrived home just shy of dawn. "I'm okay," he said.

"Well, you look like you've been run over by a tractor and left for dead." Ace blew on his hands to warm them and then shook his head. "It's that trouble with Tim Carpenter, isn't it?"

Bean said nothing, but now he appeared intrigued. Ollie, too.

Sly and his lawyer, Dave Swain, had met to discuss whether Sly should sue Carpenter. The whole idea left a bad taste in Sly's mouth. Dave didn't enjoy it either, and thought Sly should try to work things out with his neighbor, who owned the Lazy C Ranch, which was adjacent to Pettit Ranch. But Carpenter's refusal to sit down and talk had left Sly without much choice.

"I'm not happy about it," Sly said. "But that's not why I look like hell. I'm hungover."

The crew members chuckled.

"Been there more than a few times myself," Ace said. "The way you're sweatin' out that alcohol, you're sure to feel better in no time."

Sly lifted the gate of the holding pen and Ace slapped the rump of one of the January calves they'd culled from the herd earlier.

As the calf loped from the pen and Sly herded her toward

the calf table, he thought about the mess with his neighbor. Tim Carpenter had a chip on his shoulder a mile wide, mainly because Pettit Ranch was profitable. Not enough to replenish Sly's all-but-empty savings, but enough to pay the bills. It wasn't his fault the Lazy C continually struggled to stay solvent.

He and Carpenter had never been friends. Now they were enemies. All because a few months back, someone had poisoned Sly's cattle. Two of his heifers had miscarried and had lost any chance of future pregnancies, and three others had died. As a grown man, Sly rarely felt powerless, but he had then. He hated his inability to help his animals as they sickened, as he'd watched them die and feared that others could, too.

Autopsies and tests had proved that his animals had been poisoned with arsenic. Neither Sly nor his crew had any idea who'd do something so heinous. Then by chance, Ace had spotted a small pile of white powder just inside the northernmost pasture fence off the private service road that ran between Pettit Ranch and the Lazy C. He'd tested the powder and determined it to be arsenic. Both ranches shared the road, and no one else had access. Who else but Carpenter could have set the arsenic there?

Still, Sly had given his neighbor the benefit of the doubt. He'd driven to Carpenter's and attempted to question him. The first time Carpenter had ordered him off his land. On Sly's next try, he'd pulled out a rifle and aimed it at Sly's chest.

Which sure made it seem as if the man had something to hide. That was when Sly had quit trying to straighten things out himself and hired a lawyer. Not with the intention of suing, but to get Carpenter to cough up information that could shed light on what had happened. That plan had also failed, and now he really was on the verge of suing.

"Sly?" Ace was waiting for Sly to say something.

"I need to get to the bottom of this poisoning."

Ace rubbed his chin with his thumb and forefinger. "You're suing, then?"

Ollie and Bean looked down, as if the subject made them uncomfortable.

Join the crowd, Sly thought. "You all know how much those vet bills, tests and autopsies cost, and the cows we lost…" Sly shook his head. He wanted to be reimbursed for his losses.

The money he'd spent on all those things had been earmarked for a badly needed new drainage system. The existing one, installed some thirty years ago, functioned on a wing and a prayer. The next big rain could result in heavy flooding and wreak havoc on valuable low-lying pastureland. Sly and his men could do some of the grunt work, but they needed to bring in an expert. He'd considered taking out a loan to cover the costs, but as it was, the monthly payment on his mortgage was a strain. Any more debt and he'd be in over his head. He wasn't about to jeopardize everything he'd worked for by borrowing more.

"The way things stand," he said, "I don't see any other options."

"He's a tough nut to crack, all right." Ace pulled off his baseball cap and scratched one of his sideburns. "The Bitter & Sweet always brings in a live band on Friday and Saturday nights. I hope you spent some of the evening dancing off your troubles with a pretty girl."

Lana was no girl. She was all woman. "I danced a time or two," Sly admitted.

His foreman, who'd been married umpteen years, nodded approvingly. "Now and then a man's got to cut loose and have some fun."

Ollie, who knew his way around branding and, according to him, around women, too, grinned. "Me and my girl-friend, Tiff? We sure put the *f-u-n* in our Friday night." He made a lewd gesture with his hands. "But we're doin' that almost every night."

Fun didn't come close to describing Sly's night with Lana, but he wasn't about to talk about that. "Let's get this job done so Ace can take the rest of the weekend off," he said. When time and weather allowed, Sly and his foreman alternated weekends off. This was Ace's weekend, and he and his wife had planned a trip to Billings to visit their college-age son at Montana State.

"Ready with that iron?" Sly asked Ollie.

"Ready, boss."

The four of them spent the next few hours herding the calves one by one to the calf table so that the cows could be marked with the Pettit Ranch brand and then vaccinated. It wasn't exactly rocket science, allowing Sly's mind to re-play the previous evening.

Over dinner, Dave had reluctantly agreed to prepare and file the lawsuit, but he was tying up loose ends for several other clients and needed ten days to put the suit together and file the papers. Shortly after the lawyer had finished his coffee and dessert, he'd left to get home to his wife and kids.

Sly didn't have a wife or kids, or anyone to hurry home to. His life was uncomplicated, which was exactly how he liked it. He spent his days working hard to keep his ranch profitable and successful, and enjoyed spending his eve-nings either going out or relaxing alone in his quiet house. But the whole lawsuit business was unsettling, and last night he'd wanted to take his mind off his troubles. So he'd hung around the Bitter & Sweet, waiting for the band to play.

As soon as the cute blonde and her friend had sat down at a table across the way, Sly had forgotten all about his problems. He'd always enjoyed an attractive woman, and when the blonde had looked at him and smiled, something had sizzled between them. He had to meet her.

From the start, they'd hit it off. Lana was fun and easy to talk to, and her eyes had telegraphed that she was attracted to him. Best of all, she'd only wanted a good time. They'd agreed not to share their last names and had steered away from deep conversation.

A dozen dances and several drinks later, Sly had kissed her. Her warmth and enthusiasm had just about blown his socks off. Neither of them had wanted to stop, and before Sly knew it, he was walking her to the Prosperity Inn and paying for a hotel room.

Under regular circumstances he wouldn't have acted so rashly. He rarely picked up a woman he'd never met before and taken her to bed. But his decision had turned out to be a damn fine one.

The sex had been phenomenal.

His only regret was that he hadn't gotten her number. He'd thought about waking her and asking her for it before he left at the crack of dawn. But neither of them had gotten much rest, and she'd been sleeping so peacefully that he hadn't had the heart to disturb her.

Just then, Sly's daydream was interrupted when on the way to the calf table, one of the calves turned renegade and tried to run off. "Come back here, you," Sly called as he and Ace cut her off.

When they caught her and steered her back, Ace took up the conversation where they'd left off. "The gal you danced with—you gonna see her again?"

"Probably not."

The more important reason Sly hadn't asked for her number was that getting involved with her would be a bad idea. His last girlfriend had accused him of avoiding intimacy, and then dumped him. Not because she'd taken up with some other guy, but because she was fed up with his so-called emotional distance.

She wasn't the first woman to accuse him of that, but Sly had always been confused as to what "emotional distance" meant. In bed, he demonstrated plenty of emotion.

Maybe it had something do with the fact that he rarely brought the women he dated to his place. All his former girlfriends had complained about that, but hell, his home was his sanctuary and his bedroom was his private space, off-limits to all but his housekeeper, who cleaned it.

After his last breakup and a few months of self-imposed celibacy, Sly had finally figured out what women meant by emotional distance. He admitted to himself that outside the physical stuff, he'd never had a truly intimate relationship with a woman. Sure, he enjoyed giving and receiving pleasure, but he wasn't about to put his heart on the line. With good reason.

People he cared deeply about tended not to stick around. First his parents, then his brother, then the girl he'd wanted to marry.

Why take the risk of getting too close? Sly wasn't about to set himself up for that kind of heartache again.

"Now that you sweated that hangover out of your system, you're lookin' a sight better," Ace commented some hours later, when they'd finished the branding.

"I suppose I'll live," Sly replied. "Go on now and have a nice weekend—all three of you."

He headed for the house. Mrs. Rutland, his part-time housekeeper—with just him to feed and clean up after, he didn't need her full-time—left at noon on Thursdays and Fridays, but cooked enough meals to last until Monday. After showering and changing, Sly filled his belly and then headed outside again to tackle the late-afternoon chores. He fed and watered the horses, giving Bee, his bay, her usual carrot. He checked on the stock and noted additional chores that needed doing the following day.

Then he flopped on the sofa with the remote. Nothing on the tube interested him, and his mind kept wandering to last night. As worn-out as he was, he felt oddly restless—too restless to hang around at home. He considered grabbing a beer someplace, but after last night he needed a rest from alcohol.

He called his sister to ask if she wanted to catch a movie. Dani didn't answer, which wasn't surprising on a Saturday night. She was probably out with her boyfriend of the month or her friends.

Sly hung up without leaving a message. He almost wished he had Lana's number...until he reminded himself that it was better he didn't.

Moments later he grabbed his keys from the hook by the door and left through the mudroom. He wasn't sure where he was headed, but anyplace was better than sitting around here, thinking about a woman he didn't plan on ever seeing again.

It was late Sunday when Lana parked in front of the house where she'd grown up. It was a beautiful afternoon; the sun was slowly sinking toward the horizon, casting the distant, snow-covered Cascade Mountains in rosy hues. Spring was her favorite time of year, when the air smelled fresh and sweet, and life seemed to bud and surge everywhere.

Usually she looked forward to the noisy Sunday night dinners with her parents and her younger sister and family. But tonight, Lana was dreading it.

All because last Sunday, she'd finally told her parents about her decision to adopt a baby. She'd waited until two months after the social worker had cleared her as a prospective parent, and six weeks after she'd begun to actively search for a pregnant woman wanting to give up her baby for adoption. The social worker had given her the web address of a county-wide site called AdoptionOption.com, which put prospective parents in touch with pregnant teens who wanted to give up their babies. Although Lana visited the site daily, she had yet to make a contact that might work out. Discouraging, but she understood that the process would take time. Eventually she'd find someone.

Not wanting to keep such a big decision to herself, she'd told her sister first. That had been easy. Telling her parents, who tended to be old-fashioned, not so much. Lana had known they wouldn't approve. Not of adoption itself, but of her decision to adopt as a single woman.

Apprehension had ruined her appetite and she'd barely managed to eat her mother's delicious meal. She'd waited to spring her news until after dessert, when her niece and nephew had scampered off to play. She'd quickly delivered the news to her parents, then left while they were still digesting the news.

The fallout had come later, in a series of increasingly upset phone calls, one from her dad and too many to count from her mother. All of them about finding a husband and *then* adopting. With their old-fashioned values about raising kids—values Lana had supported until Brent had divorced her—they didn't understand.

"I would love to have a husband to help me raise a child, but I'm not even dating right now," she'd explained. "Besides, I'm thirty-two years old, and I know in my heart that this is the right time for me to adopt."

No amount of reasoning had changed their minds. So Lana was cringing at the prospect of another of her mother's lectures tonight. She was banking on her parents having to behave in front of their grandkids.

Which was why, knowing Liz et al usually arrived about five, Lana was pulling up to the house a little later.

Crossing her fingers for a pleasant evening free of judgment and criticism, she crossed the brick stoop, wiped her feet on the welcome mat and walked into the house. She hung her jacket on a hook by the door.

The living room was empty, but through the window that faced the backyard she noted her brother-in-law, Eric, and her father lighting what looked to be a new barbecue grill. Connor, age six, and Emma, who had just turned four, were racing around the same pint-size log cabin Lana and Liz had once played in. There was no sign of Lana's sister or their mother. They were probably working on dinner.

Lana was about to slip back out the door and head around the house to play with the kids when her sister called out. "Is that you, Lana? Mom and I are in the kitchen."

No chance of sneaking away now. "I'll be right there," Lana replied.

Shoulders squared, she headed down the hall. Liz understood Lana's aching desire to have a child, and supported her decision. Why couldn't her parents be as accepting?

She forced herself to be cheerful, declaring, "Something smells really good," as she entered the big, homey kitchen.

Her mother was sautéing mushrooms and didn't look up. "I'm just finishing the rice dish. Why don't you toss the salad, Lana?"

Not even a hello? Lana exchanged a glance with Liz, who shrugged. "Um, hi, Mom, it's nice to see you, too?"

"Hello," she said in a cool tone.

Liz scanned Lana up and down. "You look fantastic. Doesn't she, Mom?"

At last her mother turned her attention to Lana. Bracing for whatever she might say, Lana sucked in a breath.

"You are wearing a certain glow." Her mother gave her a curious stare, as in, "Where did that come from?"

This was good, much better than another criticism about choosing single motherhood. Maybe her mother had decided to lay off the awful lectures tonight. Lana crossed her fingers. And thought about the "certain glow" that apparently was still with her.

It had been almost forty-eight hours since her night with Sly. By now any afterglow should have faded. Yet inside, Lana was still purring like a satisfied cat. Turning away from her mother's and sister's curious expressions, she washed her hands. "I caught up on my sleep last night—that must be the reason," she said over the hiss of the water. "Did Dad get a new grill?"

"Yesterday, and this one has more bells and whistles than the old model—it does everything but shine shoes," her mother answered. "He's as excited as a boy on Christmas morning. He couldn't wait to show it to Eric."

"Men and their toys." Liz shook her head, her ultrashort bangs and chin-length hair making her appear twenty instead of thirty. "If I know Eric, he'll want one exactly like it, just to keep up."

"With Eric's construction business doing so well, you can certainly afford a new grill," their mother pointed out.

The kitchen door opened and Connor and Emma rushed inside. "Aunt Lana! Aunt Lana!"

They raced straight for Lana. Her heart swelling with love, she leaned down and hugged them both. She envied Liz, with her loving husband and two adorable children. "It's been a whole week since I saw you. What's new?"

"Daddy's gonna sign me up for T-ball in June," Connor said proudly. "When is that, Aunt Lana?"

"Let's see. Today is April 6," Lana said. "After April comes…?"

Connor screwed up his face. "Summer?"

Lana laughed. "Summer isn't for a little while yet, buddy. After April comes May, then June."

Emma gave an enthusiastic nod. "When I'm five, I get to play T-ball, too."

"That'll be next summer—how exciting." Lana made a mental note to get the dates of the games so she could cheer Connor on.

"How are Daddy and Grandpa doing with the hamburgers?" Liz asked.

"Good," Emma replied. "We're 'posed to tell you that they're almost ready."

"Then you'd both better hang up your jackets and wash your hands." Liz pointed to the powder room.

The men brought in the hamburgers, greeted Lana and helped set the food on the dining room table. Dinner was the usual chaotic but fun affair, with Connor and Emma causing lots of laughter.

Lana finally relaxed. She was almost home free. With any luck she would skate through the rest of the evening with a smile on her face and then head home filled with the warmth borne out of family harmony. Or so she thought.

Chapter Two

At the end of the Sunday meal, Emma and Connor scampered into the fenced backyard to play. The adults lingered at the table, sipping coffee and chatting.

"I keep forgetting to mention, I ran into Cousin Tim at the grocery yesterday," Lana's mother said.

Lana's cousin from her father's side was nine years her senior, but he seemed much older. Always a brusque man, he'd grown even more difficult after his wife had divorced him less than a year after their wedding. Having grown up in a bustling city, his ex had decided that the ranching life wasn't for her. Or maybe the problem lay with Cousin Tim himself. Lana wasn't sure. Her cousin rarely smiled or laughed, which made being around him a chore. After eleven years, it was long past time for him to get over his ex and move on.

"We haven't heard from him since last Christmas," her father said. "How is he?"

"Not so good." Her mother looked solemn. "He told me that a few months ago, some of the cows at Pettit Ranch died suddenly. It turned out they were poisoned. Sly Pettit has accused Tim."

Two men named Sly in the same town.... What were the odds? Lana had gone to high school with yet another. Apparently the name was popular among the sixty-thousand-odd residents here in Prosperity. She imagined Cousin Tim's neighbor, who she'd never met, to be as beefy and bowlegged as her cousin.

"That's terrible—unless Cousin Tim actually did it," Liz quipped. Both parents stared at her, appalled. "Well, he isn't the nicest person."

Their father frowned. "I don't care, he's family, and—"

"Family sticks together through thick and thin," Lana, Liz and Eric replied in unison.

They meant it, too—especially when times were tough. When Brent left Lana, they'd wrapped her in so much love and warmth, they'd nearly smothered her. But now that she wanted to adopt a baby by herself… Her parents' disapproval ruled out their support.

Liz made a face. "Just because the man is family doesn't mean we have to like him. He's never exactly been fond of us, either."

"Ranching is a tough business," her father said. "Tim inherited the Lazy C from your great-uncle Horace, and it never has been a moneymaker. That kind of stress would make anyone grouchy."

"Living all alone on that big ranch…" Lana's mother shook her head. "I wouldn't like that at all."

"He has a crew and foreman to keep him company," Liz pointed out.

Under her breath she muttered, "They probably can't stand him, either." Then, in her normal voice, she said, "He could sell the ranch and find a job in the city, where he'd collect a regular paycheck," Lana suggested.

"With acreage prices at record lows, this isn't the smartest time to sell," Lana's dad said. "Besides, Cousin Tim is a rancher through and through. As bitter and rough around the edges as he is, at heart he's a decent man. He wouldn't poison anyone's cows."

Lana frowned. "Then why would Mr. Pettit accuse him of such a thing?"

"God only knows, but I'm sure Tim is eager tell me all about it. I suppose I'd better call him, since he hasn't called me." Her father's heavy breath indicated it would be a chore.

"Changing the subject..." Lana said. "Remember the reporter from the *Prosperity Daily News* who took pictures of the day care and interviewed me back in early March? He's going to highlight the story as the Small Business Profile of the Month. It'll run in the paper a week from Tuesday."

Her father beamed. "That's terrific, honey. My daughter, the businesswoman. Just like your old man."

Prosperity wasn't just a ranching town. Thanks to heavily wooded areas, the Ames and Missouri Rivers, Prosperity Falls and the Cascade Mountains beyond, during spring and summer the town attracted thousands of outdoor enthusiasts. Lana's father had cashed in on those tourists with a popular recreational-equipment business that rented and sold camping, hiking and fishing gear.

"Eric's good at business, too," Liz said.

Lana's father smiled at his son-in-law. "That goes without saying. Eric, you know I'm damn proud of you, son."

Eric grinned. "I do, sir."

"You're the best, Eric," Lana said. "I never could have opened Tender Loving Daycare without your help. I had no idea how to remodel an old dance studio into a day care."

"That profile in the paper is sure to drum up business, so you'll probably need his help again soon for a second day-care center," her father said.

"I've been thinking the same thing—when the time comes." For now, Lana's main focus was finding a baby to adopt. But she wasn't going to mention that. She didn't want to set her parents off.

"That sounds exciting." Liz gave her a pleased look. "Any ideas where you'd put it?"

"Someplace downtown." Home to insurance and title companies, two banks, a library, a hospital, museums, shops, department stores and restaurants. "Think of all the people with kids who work in or around the downtown area. Wouldn't it be convenient if they could drop off their children near where they work?"

Her father nodded approvingly. "That's a great idea."

Everyone started talking excitedly, except for Lana's mother, who frowned. "You're already so busy, Lana. If you expand, you'll only be busier. I don't know why that social worker cleared you as a suitable mother when your day care takes all of your energy."

So much for steering clear of any controversy. Lana rolled her eyes. "Don't start, Mom. I've made my decision and I'm happy with it. Because I'm focusing on finding a baby, I'm not going to expand just now."

"If I was pregnant and wanted to give up my baby, I'd choose a married couple," her mother said.

Lana was determined to prove that she would be as good as any couple. "I'd make a great mom, and I'll do whatever I can to convince people that I'm the best choice."

Her mother's lips thinned. "You have enough trouble meeting men without bringing a baby into your life."

Lana's back stiffened. Her mom just wouldn't quit. "Just because I'm not dating right now doesn't mean I can't meet men." She'd had no trouble with Sly.... But they weren't going to see each other again, so she wasn't going to think about him. "As I've explained at least a dozen times, this isn't a decision I made lightly. I've been contemplating adoption for ages."

For nearly two years now, in fact, after having spent four

years trying to get pregnant, first the usual way, and then with the help of fertility drugs.

There had been nothing wrong with Brent. Lana had been the problem, the fertility doctor had explained before delivering the staggering blow that their odds of having a biological child were slim to none.

That still hurt, and always would.

Longing for a child, Lana had suggested adoption. But Brent had wanted to father his own child, and a few months after learning of Lana's inability to conceive, he'd left her for Julia.

"I've always wanted a houseful of kids," she continued. "It would be nice if I was married, but with or without a husband, I'm going to do this, and I would really appreciate your and Dad's support."

Her mother's mouth tightened. "I don't—"

To Lana's surprise, her father cut off her mother with a warning look. "Leave her alone, Michele. I'm not happy about this either, but arguing with Lana isn't going to work. She's always been single-minded about what she wants and is not afraid to go after it. It's one of the qualities that makes her a good businesswoman."

"I just want her to be happy, Chet. If she could just get over Brent…"

"I'm right here, Mom and Dad, and FYI, I'm totally over him."

To Lana's amazement, she was. Sometime in the past few days she'd stopped hurting. Come to think of it, Friday evening. Lana marveled over how she'd changed. As recklessly as she'd behaved, that night with Sly had helped her heal.

"I'm glad to hear you say that, honey," Lana's mother said. "Now that you've finally gotten Brent out of your system, why not make an effort and put yourself out there before you act on this crazy idea to adopt a baby by yourself."

As much as Lana needed her mom's support, she wasn't going to get it tonight. Unable to bear one more negative comment, she gave up—for now.

"I still have things to do tonight to get ready for tomorrow. I'm going home." Ignoring her mother's shocked expression, she stood. "Thanks for dinner."

So much for that warm, all-is-well-with-my-family feeling. She would keep moving forward with her plan and hope that in time, her parents would come around. If not, she'd go it alone.

"Will you look at that," Sly murmured as he scanned the morning paper over breakfast on a Tuesday morning in mid-April.

Mrs. Rutland, his forty-something housekeeper, stopped working on whatever she was making for dinner to peer over his shoulder. "Ah, you're reading the Small Business Profile of the Month. I read it earlier, while the coffee percolated. I've heard great things about Tender Loving Daycare, TLD for short."

"Have you," Sly said distractedly.

Because he recognized the owner of the business from the photo accompanying the article. It was Lana, the woman he couldn't seem to stop thinking about. Even now, more than a week after their night together, a mere glance at her smile caused his body to stir.

Hell, just imagining her did that.

After a week, he realized he wanted to get to know her. Nothing serious or long-term, but a chance to explore their attraction.

Now he had her full name. Lana Carpenter. Sly grimaced at that. He hoped she wasn't related to Tim Carpenter, the man he was suing. According to the attorney, Carpenter should receive the notice sometime today.

"These monthly profiles put small businesses on the Prosperity map, both for us locals and the tourists," Mrs. R said. "With hundreds of businesses to choose from, I think it's wonderful that the *Daily News* picked a day care this time. You don't have any kids yet, Sly, but someday you will. Maybe you'll send them to TLD."

Sly had already raised a kid—his brother, Seth. And look how that had turned out. The experience had soured him on having his own children. He'd have to be nuts to put himself—or some poor kid—through that again.

He went back to the article, his eyes on the photo. Lana looked happy and beautiful, as did the boys and girls gathered around her. But, hell, if she had her arms around Sly the way she did around those little ones, he'd be grinning just as widely.

"How do you know about the day care, Mrs. R?" he asked. "Your son and daughter are grown. When they were little, Lana Carpenter was probably in day care herself."

"A couple of my kids' friends take their children to TLD. They're always talking about how great Lana Carpenter is. She has a special way with children. They love her."

She also had other special ways, private things that made a man wild. Sly's body hardened. He wished he could stop thinking about her, but so far he hadn't had much luck with that.

Which was why he'd decided to see her again, casually. He'd returned to the Bitter & Sweet last Friday night in case she was there.

She wasn't. He'd danced with a couple of different women, both of them signaling that they were open to more than dancing. But neither could compare to beautiful, funny, sexy Lana, and after an hour or so, he'd left.

Hands on her ample hips, Mrs. Rutland looked worried. "Is something wrong with your omelet?"

Sly realized he was frowning. He curled his mouth into a smile. "It's real good." He glanced at his watch and was surprised to discover how late it was. "I told Ace I'd help him and the others move part of the herd today," he said as he shoveled in big bites. "I'd best finish and get out there."

COUNTING LABOR, FENCING, feed and vet care, cattle cost a bundle to raise, nearly three thousand dollars per animal per year. Growing his own summer and fall pasture grass cut down on food costs, and the nutrient-rich crop helped keep the animals strong and healthy. But in winter and spring, Sly relied on vitamin and mineral supplements for that. Supplies were running low, so late Tuesday afternoon he headed out to pick up more, as well as a roll of barbwire for the fences, which always seemed to need mending. But instead of turning east toward Drysdale's Ranching and Farm Supplies, he headed west.

Before he knew it, he was driving along River Drive, a pretty street that followed the Ames River through town and ended at Prosperity Park and the awesome Prosperity Falls. The cascading waterfall was a popular site for marriage proposals and outdoor weddings, and drew visitors from all over.

Miles before reaching the park, though, Sly turned off, onto Hawthorn Road. The colorful Tender Loving Daycare sign immediately drew his attention. So this was Lana's day care. He slowed way down to study the square clapboard building. Painted a soft green, it had purple shutters and window boxes. April was too early for flowers in the boxes, so colorful windmills stood in their stead. On one side of the building, a big fenced yard marked a kids' paradise of swings and slides and all sorts of climbing toys. On the other was a parking lot.

Sly had to find out if the attraction between them was as strong as he remembered, so he pulled in, noting that the lot was empty except for a minivan, a light green sedan and his truck. But then, it was after six. Sly was debating whether to go inside or take off, when the door opened. Amy Simmons—no, Amy Watkins now—sauntered through it holding the hand of a pint-size little girl. Lana followed behind them without a coat, as if she didn't expect to stay out long.

Amy noticed him right away. "Well, hello there," she said, approaching him with a dazzling smile. "What brings you here?"

Sly had no choice but to slide out of the truck. "Hey, Amy." He nodded at Lana. "I'm here to see her."

Lana had moved to stand beside Amy, her eyes wide with surprise. "Sly—uh, hi," she said.

Amy gave them both speculative looks. "I didn't realize you two knew each other."

They knew each other, all right, in ways that would make Amy blush if she realized.

Lana met his gaze, her green eyes warning him to say nothing about how they'd met. He gave a subtle nod, then smiled at the girl peering from behind Amy's knees. "Is that your little girl, Amy?"

"Yes, this is Courtney. She's three now." Amy scooped up her daughter and kissed her. "Say hi to Sly, sweetie."

The girl giggled. "Hi, Thly."

She was about the cutest thing Sly had ever seen. "Hey there, Courtney." He patted her head. "How's married life?" he asked Amy.

"I'm enjoying it. Jon and I are having so much fun with Courtney that we're having another baby in the fall." She touched her softly rounded abdomen. "Well, I'd better get this little one home. See you tomorrow, Lana, and thanks for keeping her a few minutes late." Amy flashed a sly smile. "You two have fun."

"How did you and Amy meet?" Lana asked as the woman buckled her daughter into her car seat.

Sly watched the minivan roll out of the parking lot. "We dated years ago." Amy had wanted to get serious, but he hadn't and they'd broken up. "Coming here now is bad timing on my part," he added. "She's a big gossip."

"Tell me about it." Lana fiddled with the cuff of her blouse, her expression both curious and openly pleased that he was there. "How did you find me, and what are you doing here?"

"I saw your business profile in the paper. Great article." He dug his copy from the hip pocket of his jeans and handed it to her. "In case you didn't get a hard copy."

"Thanks, Sly."

As she took it from him, her fingers casually brushed his. Heat shot straight to his groin, and by the sudden flush of her cheeks, she, too, felt the powerful connection between them. Yes, the pull between them was as strong as he remembered.

He cleared his throat. "I didn't get a chance to say goodbye before I left you that morning."

"I'm glad you let me sleep in. Oh, and thanks for the aspirin. It helped."

"No problem."

Silence.

In the uncomfortable moments that stretched between them, Lana glanced over her shoulder at the day-care door, as if she wanted to slip through it. "I—"

"You—" he said at the same time, then paused. "Go ahead," Sly insisted.

"I want you to know that I usually don't spend the night with a man I just met. You were the first and the last."

"I'm honored that you picked me. I enjoyed our night together."

Her warm eyes flashed that she had, too. She had a mouth made for loving. Plump, soft lips that were naturally pink. They parted a fraction, just as they had seconds before he'd kissed her on the night they'd spent together.

Sly definitely wanted to explore that heat, unleash her fiery passion and enjoy a repeat of their memorable night together. He moved closer and tucked her hair behind her ears with hands that shook.

He wanted her that much. Too much.

The strength of his need scared him. If he was smart, he'd turn around and leave. But his legs refused to budge.

Finally Lana swallowed and backed up a step. "Is there anything else you wanted?"

Besides kissing her and more? At the moment Sly couldn't think of a thing. He was debating whether to ask her out or walk away while he still could when she spoke.

"Okay, then," she said. "It's chilly out here and I left my coat inside. I also need to get ready for tomorrow. Thanks again for the article."

She left him standing in the parking lot, feeling both relieved and confused.

Clearly he'd misread her. She wasn't so happy to see him after all.

Actually, that made sense. He wasn't supposed to think about her and he sure wasn't supposed seek her out. They'd agreed on that.

Yet here he was standing in the parking lot of the business she owned, aching for her, even though getting involved with her could be dangerous.

What the hell was wrong with him?

Chapter Three

Lana made a practice of responding to TLD emails by the end of the same day she received them. She usually took care of that chore before leaving work, but thanks to Sly, today she'd been too rattled.

If that wasn't enough, her father had called to say that Cousin Tim was being sued by his neighbor. No one in the family had ever been sued, and they all were upset and banding around Cousin Tim. They offered to be character witnesses, lend him money for an attorney and whatever else he needed. Cousin Tim was too proud to accept their money, but said he'd let them know if character witnesses would help.

Still a little flummoxed, Lana stood in the kitchen, waiting for the kettle to whistle so that she could make a cup of herbal tea. For days now, she'd tried to push the night with Sly from her mind, without much success. She assured herself that she'd eventually forget the handsome cowboy who dominated her waking thoughts. She certainly hadn't expected to see him again, and had been both surprised and elated when he'd shown up at the day care.

But her feelings had quickly turned to disappointment. Sly hadn't asked for her phone number or a date. He hadn't asked her a single question or said more than a sentence or two. In fact, he hadn't seemed interested in getting to know her at all, or wanting her to know anything about him. Instead, his heavy-lidded expression had told her exactly what he wanted.

More of what they'd shared on that wild night.

Against Lana's better judgment, she'd wanted that, too. The attraction between them was more potent than anything she'd ever experienced, even during her honeymoon days with Brent. To the point that when Sly had moved close to her, her mind had all but emptied.

She frowned. How could she feel so strongly about a man she'd just met? She had no idea what his last name was or whether he really was a rancher, where he worked or anything about his family. Although she had a hunch that Amy would fill her in tomorrow when she picked up Courtney after work.

At last the kettle whistled, and Lana pushed Sly from her mind. Tonight she had better things to do than fantasize about the sexy cowboy. She carried her steaming mug to her home office, which doubled as the den.

The only positive thing about his visit this afternoon was that he'd distracted her from dwelling on the lack of interest her profile had generated at AdoptionOption.com. With input from the social worker, Lana had carefully created the online profile with her photo and other information. Although many girls had contacted her, nothing had stuck.

Lana wished she could figure out why. Was it because she was single, or something else? The lack of any serious interest was discouraging, and she wished she'd waited to share her decision with her family until she'd formed a promising relationship with an expectant mother.

Not about to give up, she decided tonight she'd check the website after she checked her email. She sat down and scrolled through her inbox. There were ten—ten!—inquiries from parents who'd read the profile in the paper and wanted to visit TLD. Her friend Kate had also emailed, whining about an upcoming blind date her mother had orchestrated. Several other friends had sent the usual jokes and gossip.

But one email stood out. "Baby," the subject line read, from Sophie@AdoptionOption.com. Hardly daring to breathe, Lana opened the email.

I got your name from the AdoptionOption website. I'm Sophie and I'm four months pregnant. I'm looking for the right person to adopt my baby. When I saw the article about you in the paper today and read your online profile at the website, I couldn't believe it. You seem to really care about kids, and I would like to meet you. Text me at 406-555-2223.

This was the chance Lana had waited, hoped and prayed for. Sucking in an excited breath, she jotted down the number with shaky hands.

Yet as badly as she longed for a baby, she had to admit that she was also a little scared. Raising a child without a partner was going to be a huge job.

Too antsy to sit, she paced to the window and looked out. Despite the lights from the other town houses and the shade tree in her yard, she could see the crescent moon and the stars studding the sky like diamonds. Tonight they seemed especially bright. Lana took that as a good omen.

Regardless of the challenges ahead, she wanted a child with all her heart. She wasn't about to let this opportunity pass by. She grabbed her cell phone and texted the girl.

Hi, I would love to get together. How about Big Mama's— my treat. Tell me when and I'll be there. Looking forward to meeting you,
Lana

She'd chosen Big Mama's Café because everyone loved the restaurant's food. Less than a minute later, Sophie texted back. Saturday @ 10?

Gleeful, Lana replied. Sounds perfect. I'm 5'6" and have longish blond hair.

Sophie texted. I know what u look like from yr profile and the pic in the paper. CU.

A baby of her own!

"Don't get ahead of yourself," Lana cautioned out loud.

Sophie might decide she wasn't the right person to raise her child, and allowing herself to imagine otherwise would only set her up for heartache.

Still, she was too excited to worry about that now, or to read the other emails. She logged in to AdoptionOption. com and checked Sophie's profile. The girl was sixteen and a junior at Jupiter High School on the far side of town. She had short hair, dyed white-blond with neon-pink streaks and bangs that fell into big, soulful eyes lined in thick eye pencil. Despite the alternative look, she was very pretty, and Lana guessed that the baby would be beautiful.

"She's not the mother of my child yet," she reminded herself.

Not that it calmed her down. Laughing, she danced around the room while she speed-dialed Kate. After three rings, her friend answered.

"It's happened," Lana said, skipping the usual pleasantries.

"You have a blind date, too? Ugh. You know that sewing circle my mom belongs to? That's where it happened. I cannot believe she went behind my back and fixed me up with her friend's sister's son. That sounds like a really bad joke, doesn't it? Too bad it's real. Save me, please."

The whole thing *did* sound awful. Lana's mother had her faults, but she wouldn't set up a blind date without first checking with Lana. Bonus points for her. "You never know," Lana said. "It could work out."

"With the son of the sister of some woman in my mom's sewing circle? Puh-leeze. You said *it* happened. Don't tell me Sly finally found you."

"He did, but this is about a baby. Tonight I got an email from a pregnant girl who saw the article on TLD in the paper." Lana squeezed her eyes shut and squealed. "She wants to meet me."

"Wow, that's great. But back up a minute. Did you say that Sly found you? I knew he would! Why didn't you phone me?" Kate sounded hurt.

"Because it happened late this afternoon, and I haven't had a chance to call until now."

"I want details."

"Okay, but first let me fill you in about Sophie—the pregnant girl."

"Believe me, I want to hear all about her. After you spill on what happened with Sly."

Realizing Kate wouldn't let up until she got the information she wanted, Lana threw up her hand. "All right, but there isn't much to say. He read my business profile in the paper. That's how he learned where I work."

"That piece was terrific, by the way, and look at the results you're already seeing. A pregnant girl contacts you and Sly shows up at the day care. Why can't they run an article about *me* in the paper?"

"Start your own business and it just might happen."

"I like managing the Treasures Gift Shop at Prosperity Falls just fine, thanks. Back to Sly. What did he say, and what did you say?"

"He apologized for leaving the morning after without a goodbye." He'd seemed so sincere and contrite that Lana had almost melted. "And he brought me a copy of the news-paper article."

"What a sweetheart. When are you two going out?"

"He didn't ask me out," Lana said. "I never had a chance to find out his last name or anything else about him. He was only interested in kissing me."

"Ooh. Did you let him?"

"Of course not." But Lana had wanted to. Badly.

"Are you crazy? If you don't want to kiss Sly Whatever-his-last-name-is, send him my way."

"Ha, ha, ha. I didn't let him kiss me because he's only interested in one thing."

"I thought you liked doing that one thing with him."

Lana gritted her teeth. "You're not helping, Kate. I don't want a sex-only relationship. I want more than that." Especially now, when she just might have a chance at a baby....

She wanted a relationship based on shared mutual interests and honest conversation, things that formed a basis for something that lasted. True, those very things had failed to hold her marriage together, but that was because Brent had found her lacking.

"But he's so darned hot," Kate said. "And he seemed very into you that night...."

She was right on both counts. Sly had seemed just as into Lana today, but not in the way she wanted. "If he was that interested, he'd have at least asked for my phone number."

"You mean, he didn't?"

"Nope. Unfortunately, his attraction to me is purely sexual."

"Bummer," Kate said. "Just once, I'd like to meet a man interested in getting to know me before he tries to jump my bones. You keep saying he's out there. If he is, I sure haven't met him."

"Yeah, well, I haven't found my Mr. Right, either." Lana

had thought she had with Brent, but he'd turned out to be Mr. Wrong instead. "Wouldn't it be funny if your blind date turns out to be 'the one'?"

Kate snorted. "Don't hold your breath. Now tell me about the pregnant girl."

"Her name is Sophie, and we're meeting Saturday at Big Mama's. I'm treating her to brunch."

"How exciting! I'll keep my fingers crossed for you. Good luck."

"Do you think I need luck?" Lana bit her lip.

"It's just a figure of speech. Be yourself, and Sophie will love you, like everyone else who knows you."

More than anything in the world, Lana hoped her friend was right.

"So, Lana, how long have you and Sly been dating?" Amy asked when she arrived to pick up Courtney on Wednesday afternoon.

Amy was a great mom, but as Sly had pointed out the other day, she was also a big gossip. Lana was glad that her two assistants had gone home for the day and that only she, Amy and another mom named Sheila were at the day care. "Actually, we're not dating," she said.

Amy lifted a skeptical eyebrow. "Sly sure didn't stop by yesterday to pick up a child. He doesn't have kids of his own, or any nieces or nephews that I'm aware of. He said he was here to see you."

In the act of helping her four-year-old son with his jacket, Sheila widened her eyes. "You must be talking about Sly Pettit. He was here?"

Amy grinned. "In the flesh."

Wait. Sly *Pettit*—the rancher who was suing Cousin Tim? Lana tried not to show her shock.

"What's wrong, Lana?" Sheila asked.

"I'm just surprised that you both know him."

"We certainly do," Amy said with a smirk. "We both used to date him, though not at the same time. I haven't seen him in a good four years, and he's still as gorgeous as ever," she told Sheila. "I'm guessing he's still a heart-breaker, too."

Sheila zipped her son's jacket and directed him to get his lunch box. "We dated about six years ago. By our second or third date I was head over heels for him. I was sure I'd be the one to snag him." She gave her head a sad shake. "Unfortunately he didn't feel the same way about me. I couldn't even get him to show me his ranch. After a few months, we broke up."

Amy nodded. "My story is similar. Sly showed me the ranch, but only because I asked. I'd heard that his bedroom was off-limits to the women he dated, but I always hoped I'd be the one he fell for, the one he'd invite to his bed. He never did—we always ended up at my place. I tried everything to make him love me, but no luck." She let out a sigh, followed by a shrug. "I guess I ended up lucky after all. I met and married Jon, and we're so happy."

"Sly has dated a lot of women and broken a lot of hearts," Sheila said. "Be careful, Lana."

"Thanks for the warning," Lana said, but she wasn't worried. She and Sly weren't dating, and now they never would.

Not with him suing her cousin.

SLY AND HIS sister, Dani, were close, and as busy as they both were with their jobs, they made sure they got together a couple times a month. On Wednesday night they met at Clancy's, a bar and pool hall south of town. Clancy's was always crowded, but boasted a dozen pool tables—enough so that he and Dani were usually able to snag one.

"I met a woman," Sly told his sister over the loud country-and-western music adding to the noise. He hadn't planned on saying anything and wasn't sure why he'd made the confession. Especially when lately, he hadn't dated much and she'd been bugging him about it. Now she'd *really* bug him.

But Lana… Sly was still thinking about her, even though she'd shut him down. There was something about her, and he needed to tell somebody.

In the middle of placing the balls, Dani swiveled her head his way. "Oh?" Her eyes, the same silver-blue as Sly's and Seth's, sparked with curiosity.

Not wanting to make a big deal out of what he'd said, he tugged on her ponytail like he had when she was four. Before life had knocked them both upside the head.

"Stop that." Hiding a smile, she batted his hand away. "I'm not a little girl anymore. I'm twenty-eight years old."

Dani was seven years younger than him, and one of the few people he trusted. He flashed a grin. "You'll always be my baby sister, even when you're fifty."

"By then you'll be an old man, and probably too frail to pull my hair."

Sly scowled, but Dani thought that was real funny. "I'll take solid, you take the stripes," she said.

While she eyeballed the table, aimed her cue and broke the balls, Sly thought about how far they'd come since he was eleven and their mother had died. Two years later their father had followed her, leaving them orphans. Sly had wanted to take care of his siblings, but he'd been too young.

Their only family had been an uncle Sly and his siblings had never met, a man who lived in Iowa. Uncle George had grudgingly taken in Sly and his younger brother, Seth, who was ten at the time, but he hadn't wanted Dani.

She'd entered the foster-care system in Prosperity. Sly

had worried about her constantly and vowed that someday he would reunite their little family.

But it turned out that he and Seth had gotten the raw end of that stick. Their uncle had disliked kids and had mostly ignored him and Seth, which was better than the alternative. His idea of attention had been to yell and raise his hand. Sly and his brother had quickly learned to steer clear of him.

Sly had become his brother's caretaker and parent of sorts, raising Seth as best he could. His best hadn't been so great, though. A kid with an independent streak, Seth had fought him on everything. By the time Uncle George had died just before Sly's eighteenth birthday, his relationship with his brother had deteriorated badly. Hoping that returning home and reuniting with Dani would help mend the damages, Sly had brought his brother back to Prosperity. Unfortunately, nothing had changed. After several minor scrapes with the law, Seth had dropped out of high school and left town. A few months later, Sly and Dani had received a postcard letting them know he'd settled in California. He'd failed to provide the name of the city, and the postal stamp had been impossible to decipher. Seth hadn't spoken to or contacted them since.

Dani had ended up with a much better deal. Big Mama, her foster mom, had loved her from the start and eventually had adopted her.

Dani hit the ball into a side pocket. Another ball slid into a different pocket. She did a little dance. "Dang, I'm good."

"Cocky, too," Sly teased. "Wait until it's my turn."

She missed the next shot. Sly chalked his cue. "Watch and learn, little sister." He took aim and dropped a striped ball into the corner pocket. He put away four more, then missed.

Before Dani took aim, she angled her head at him. "I'm

glad to hear you met someone, big brother. How and where did it happen?"

"Remember that dinner meeting with my lawyer a couple weeks ago at the Bitter & Sweet? She was there with a girlfriend. We ended up dancing the whole night."

"The *whole* night?"

Sly wasn't about to answer that. "Are you ever going to move that cue?"

Dani ignored him. "Her girlfriend must've been bored silly."

"Yeah. She went home." Sly nudged her aside. "I'll shoot for you."

"No way." She gave him a friendly poke in the ribs. "Does this woman have a name?"

"Lana Carpenter." The words rolled off Sly's tongue and left a sweet taste in his mouth.

"That sounds familiar. Where have I heard of Lana Carpenter?" Dani wondered, tapping the cue with her finger. "I don't think she's one of my regulars."

Dani worked at Big Mama's Café, a popular place open for breakfast and lunch that Big Mama had started some thirty years earlier. Someday when Big Mama retired, the restaurant would be Dani's.

His sister finally took her shot, pocketed one and missed the next shot. "Shoot," she grumbled. "You're up. Is Lana related to Tim Carpenter?"

Sly sure as hell hoped not. "Haven't asked her."

"She doesn't know you're thinking about suing a man who could be related to her?"

"I'm definitely suing." Sly was still unhappy about having to take legal action. He missed his shot, too. "He should have gotten the papers yesterday."

"I'm sorry it had to come to that." Dani made a face. "Have you heard anything back?"

"It's all going through my lawyer. When he hears, he'll call."

She nodded. "Where does Lana Carpenter work?"

"She owns a business called Tender Loving Daycare."

"Now I remember where I've heard her name. Her day care was profiled as small business of the month in the paper. Customers have been talking about it a lot. Her picture was in the paper. She's pretty." Dani gave him a speculative look. "So where are you taking her this weekend?"

Sly almost told her about stopping by the day care to see Lana, but he didn't want to stir up his sister's curiosity any more than it already was. "We're not dating," he said.

"Why the heck not?"

Because something told Sly that Lana was the one woman who could cut right past his defenses. He wasn't about to let anyone do that.

"Let me get this straight," his sister said when he didn't answer. "The weekend before last you danced the night away with Lana Carpenter. Now you mentioned her to me, but you haven't asked her out. You must like her a lot."

Sly snorted and shook his head, but Dani had a point. He did like Lana. No, he lusted after her. It was easy to confuse the two, but he knew the difference. "I'm getting awful hungry," he said. "Let's finish this game and then grab a couple of burgers. The winner treats."

"You're on." Dani lined up her cue and shot. The ball sailed neatly into a pocket. She missed the next one. "Why haven't you asked her out?"

Darn, his sister could be a pit bull about some things. He should have figured she wasn't through with the subject of Lana Carpenter just yet. "I don't have her number," Sly said.

"That's what phone books and the internet are for."

"Things are pretty busy at the ranch."

"Excuses, excuses."

Sly took his shot and missed. He swore softly. "I missed that because I'm half starved to death."

"As soon as I sink the eight ball, I'll let you buy me that burger." The remaining solid balls disappeared into the pockets. Dani eyeballed the table. "Eight ball, corner pocket." After lining up the cue, she executed the shot perfectly. Her fists shot into the air. "Hot damn—I won!"

"I'll beat you next time," Sly said. "I keep meaning to ask—how's that guy you're dating?"

"You mean Cal?" Her smile faded. "We broke up on Sunday."

"Can't say I'm sorry." His sister seemed to gravitate toward guys who treated her poorly. "You want me to punch him for you?" He was kidding, but if she wanted him to, he'd do it.

"Absolutely not." She made a face. "I'm a big girl, Sly. I can take care of myself. I just wish that I could meet a guy and have something that lasted more than a couple of months."

Sly hoped she found what she wanted. So far, she hadn't had much luck. "You and I are alike that way—both of us suck at relationships."

"Sad but true." She gave him a somber look. "The difference between us is that I *want* to find someone, get married and have kids. You don't."

Sly shrugged. "I'm happy the way I am."

"Well, I'm tired of going home to my apartment and cooking for one. It gets lonely."

Another voice cut in—a lowlife named Paul. "Hey, Dani. Sly."

He gave Dani a blatantly sexual look that made Sly see red. He managed a terse nod.

His sister perked up. "Down, big brother," she murmured for his ears only. "Remember, I can take care of myself.

Besides, I happen to have a little crush on that cowboy." She tossed Paul a flirty smile. "Hi. What are you up to?"

"Lookin' for you. Can I buy you a beer?"

Dani glanced at Sly. "Rain check on that burger?"

"Do I have a choice?"

"Not really. Hey, why don't you come to Big Mama's for lunch on Saturday, my treat." She stood on her toes and kissed Sly's cheek.

"You won the game. I'm supposed to treat you."

"But I'm standing you up for Paul. Leave me a big tip on Saturday and we'll call it even."

"If that's how you want it." Sly resisted the urge to tug on her ponytail again. "You want me to wait around and give you a ride home?"

"I'll drive her home," Paul said, giving Dani a winning smile.

"I'd appreciate that." She took his arm and winked over her shoulder at Sly. "I'll see you Saturday."

Chapter Four

Saturday morning, Lana and Sophie sat at a booth by the window in Big Mama's Café. Locals and tourists loved the busy restaurant, which served great food and was always packed on weekends.

Big Mama's Sinfully Satisfying Frittata, a favorite of Lana's created by Big Mama herself, sat on the table in front of her, slowly growing cold. Having been up since dawn without eating a thing, she should have been famished. Instead, her stomach felt queasy. Nerves, and they showed. Usually she had no problem meeting new people and making decent conversation, but sitting here with Sophie, she couldn't come up with a single thing to say.

If only she were as calm as the girl, who was devouring her cheese-and-bacon omelet as if she hadn't eaten in days. She looked just like her profile picture, and was on the thin side, with a lean, boyish shape…until you saw her rounded belly. A snug black Mumford & Sons Live! T-shirt hugged her torso and emphasized her condition. At four months along, she definitely looked pregnant.

She stopped eating to shoot Lana a quizzical glance. "What are you smiling at?"

"When my sister was pregnant, she ate like you—as if she had hollow legs."

"I've always eaten a lot, only I wasn't fat before."

"You're not fat now—you're pregnant."

"Well, I feel fat." Sophie slathered a cinnamon roll with butter. "Why aren't you eating your food?"

Though Lana had never been less hungry in her life, she forced herself to take a bite of the frittata. "It's delicious."

After that, the conversation died.

"You're not at all like your photos," Sophie said after a moment.

"Is that good or bad?"

"It's just different. In the pictures you wore pants and a shirt. Now you're wearing a dress with little blue-and-white hearts all over it."

Wanting to make a positive impression, Lana had spent almost half an hour deciding what to wear. She'd chosen the dress because it was fairly new and she felt pretty in it. Now she wondered if she'd gone too formal. "A dress is bad?"

"Well, no, but why wear one when you don't have to?" Sophie wrinkled her nose, causing her tiny silver nose ring to stick out.

"Normally I wear jeans on weekends. In fact, I was wearing my favorites earlier. But I cleaned house this morning, which I do every Saturday," Lana explained, wanting Sophie to know she kept a tidy home. "Since this is our first meeting, I wanted to wear something a little nicer."

Sophie gave a slow nod and polished off the cinnamon roll. "I clean the apartment where my mom I and live on Saturdays, too. She works fifty hours a week for us, and it's only right that I do my part. That's what she says anyway."

Lana nodded. "That seems fair."

"I guess."

Lana racked her brain for something else to say. "Do you have an after-school job?"

"Not every day. I work part-time at the movie theater near the apartment. I take tickets and collect trash from under the seats. My shift is five to ten on Thursdays and Fridays, and one to ten on Saturdays. That's how I met Jason. He works in the concession area."

"I'm guessing Jason is the baby's father?" Lana asked.

Sophie nodded. "He doesn't want to be a father, just like I don't want to be a mom. We're too young. Now that I'm pregnant, he makes me go straight home after work to get my rest." She eyed Lana's frittata. "Are you going to eat the rest of that?"

"It's all yours. Jason sounds like a sweet guy."

"Sometimes. Last night he gave his two-week notice. He just got a new job at the candy store at the mall."

The girl's carefully blank face made Lana wonder. "Is everything okay with you two?"

"We sort of broke up last night," Sophie said to her empty plate.

She was obviously hurting. Lana felt bad for her. "I'm sorry," she said. "Breaking up is never fun."

Sophie picked at her nail. "I was getting tired of him anyway." She gave Lana a sideways look. "Did you and your boyfriend break up, too?"

"At the moment, I don't have a boyfriend and I'm not dating anyone, but I used to be married."

"Did he cheat on you? That's what my mom's last boy-friend did."

There was no reason to sugarcoat the truth. "As a matter of fact, he did," Lana said. "He wanted a baby, and when we found out that I couldn't give him one, he found a woman who could."

"That's really jacked up. Is that why you want to adopt—because you can't have a baby of your own?"

Lana nodded. "I love children, and I'm so ready to be a mother. I know I'll make a really great one." Another long silence. "Tell me what you want to be someday."

"I'm not sure. Maybe a cosmetologist like my mom. She makes decent money."

"That's a great career."

The waitress, a friendly woman named Dani, stopped at the table with a coffeepot. "Ready for your coffee now?"

Lana considered asking for the check instead and putting an end to the uncomfortable meeting. But she wanted a chance to end on a more upbeat note. She smiled. "That depends on Sophie. Do you want something else to drink?"

The girl cast a wistful gaze at the coffeepot. "Coffee, but now that I'm pregnant, I'm not supposed to."

"How about cocoa?" Dani asked. "We make ours home-made and it's excellent."

"Yeah, sure."

"I'll have that, too," Lana said.

"Two cocoas it is." For the first time, Dani really looked at Lana. "You're the woman in the paper. Lana Carpenter."

"That's right."

"It's very nice to meet you."

When Dani left, Sophie was grinning. "You're kind of a celebrity."

"Am I?" Lana laughed. "I never thought of myself that way."

"You are. Because of your picture with that story, people know you." Sophie fiddled with her napkin, then squinted slightly at Lana. "Can I ask you something?"

"Anything."

"Do you ever wish you had a boyfriend?"

Lana's mind flashed to Sly. Now, there was a terrible choice for a boyfriend—as Amy and Sheila had pointed out. Lana hadn't heard from him since he'd stopped by the day care several days ago. He wasn't boyfriend material. Even worse, he was suing her cousin. At the very thought, she felt cold and sick at heart. Angry, too. Cousin Tim wasn't the nicest person, but killing Sly's cattle? No way would he do that.

"Occasionally I get lonely," she admitted. "But most of the time I'm fine by myself. Between the day care and home projects, I keep pretty busy. Now I want to ask *you* something." She cupped her hands around her water glass and waited for Sophie's nod. "How do you feel about a single woman raising your baby?"

"It's no big deal." The girl shrugged. "That's how my mom raised me."

And here she was, a junior in high school and pregnant. Lana silently vowed to closely supervise her child throughout his or her teen years—provided she got the chance to be a mother.

"Do you ever see your dad?" Lana asked.

The girl shook her head. "My mom isn't even sure who he is."

Sophie seemed okay with that, but Lana was sad for her. She couldn't imagine not knowing her own father. *And what about my baby's father?* Lana was counting on her dad to help make up for that. Her parents weren't supporting her decision right now, but she wasn't going to lose hope. Once she had the baby, surely they'd rally. After all, she was family, and her baby would be, too.

"You should know that I'm planning to bring my child to work with me every day, and when he or she is old enough—let's call the baby a she for now—I'll enroll her in my day care. Then when she starts kindergarten, I'll cut back my hours so I can be with her after school."

"But if you do that, you'll make less money. My mom has always worked ten hours a day."

Lana nodded. "Money is important, but to me, being there for my child is even more important. I have savings that will allow me to work a little less."

The girl appeared thoughtful. "I would have liked for

my mom to be around when I got home from school. I could tell you'd make a good mom when I read the article. It's why I picked you and Mr. and Mrs. Anderson as my top two choices."

"I'm not the only person you're considering?" Lana said, her voice squeaking.

She should have guessed as much, had cautioned herself to not make any assumptions. But she'd been so excited, so sure that today's meeting would be perfect and that Sophie would like her, that the idea of other potential parents had never entered her mind.

Dani returned with the cocoas. Unaware of the utter chaos her announcement had caused inside Lana, Sophie glugged down a great deal of her drink before replying, "My social worker said I should talk to more than one person so that I can make the best choice. I'm having lunch with the Andersons tomorrow, at Baker's."

An upscale restaurant with fancy food that cost twice what it did at Big Mama's, Baker's was sure to impress the girl. "That's um, nice," Lana said.

"I've never eaten there before, have you?"

"Once or twice, for special occasions."

"Is it okay for me to wear jeans and a T-shirt?"

"I wouldn't."

Another uncomfortable silence followed.

As Lana sipped her cocoa, she had the strangest sense that someone was staring at her. She glanced out the window. Someone *was*. Sly was standing on the sidewalk right in front of her.

Sophie followed her gaze. "Wow, he's cute—for an old guy. You said you didn't have a boyfriend."

"I don't."

"He's sure looking at you the way a boyfriend would. And he's coming into the restaurant."

SLY COULDN'T BELIEVE that Lana was sitting in a booth at Big Mama's Café. Not the fact that she was eating there—everyone did—but because she was here now, on the day Dani expected him for lunch.

As usual, the place was packed with the Saturday crowd. There were no empty tables, and no sign of Big Mama. But then, she often took weekends off, handing the reins to Dani.

Naomi, the weekend hostess, smiled and tossed her head seductively. "Hey, Sly," she drawled with a sexy smile. She was a flirt, but it was all harmless fun. "Dani said you'd be coming in. I just freshened my makeup, and I sure am glad I did."

He gave her a grin. "With or without makeup, you're beautiful to me, Naomi. Add my name to the list for a table in Dani's area, will you?"

"You know it, sugar, but it could be a while."

"No problem. I'm in no hurry."

Sly greeted a couple of ranchers he was friendly with, then, hardly aware of what he was doing, wandered over to Lana's booth. She was sitting with a skinny girl with rock-band hair. Sly pegged her to be about fifteen or sixteen.

"Hey," he said.

Lana glanced up at him. In a dress sprinkled with little hearts and feminine lace on the cuffs of her short sleeves, she looked innocent and sweet. Also confused. "Hello, Sly. What are you doing here?"

"This is where my sister works. I came to see her and grab lunch."

Dani bustled right over. "Hi, big brother." She tugged him down and kissed his cheek. "We're a little short on tables right now. But hey, if Lana doesn't mind, maybe you can join her and her friend."

Lana's expression turned puzzled. "What makes you think your brother and I know each other?"

"The way you look at each other. But also because the last time I saw him, he mentioned you."

Sly was going to kill his sister.

A telltale flush crept up Lana's face. "You didn't say anything earlier, Dani."

"I wasn't sure I should. In case my brother forgot to mention it, he enjoyed his evening with you."

"You said you weren't dating anyone." The teenage girl widened her eyes dramatically at Lana. "I don't mind if he sits down with us. There's plenty of room next to Lana."

Lana gave the girl a what-are-you-up-to look before she sighed. "Okay, until a table opens up." She scooted toward the far end of the bench, leaving a good foot and a half of space for him.

"You want coffee while you're waiting for your burger, Sly? I just made a fresh pot."

"Sounds good."

"Be right back." Dani hurried off.

A frown tugged Lana's mouth.

"I only told her that you and I danced," Sly explained.

The teenage girl was staring at him. "You and Lana danced? I wish I could have seen that." She said it as if she couldn't believe people their age did that kind of thing.

"I don't believe we've met." He extended his hand. "I'm Sly."

"Cool name. I'm Sophie."

"Nice to meet you. Are you Lana's little sister?"

The girl looked at him like he was crazy. "No," she said with a smirk. "Lana and I just met today."

Interesting. "Then you must be interviewing for a job at her day care."

"Not that, either." Sophie smoothed her T-shirt over her

rounded belly. "I'm pregnant and I'm thinking I might pick Lana to adopt my baby."

Lana seemed to catch her breath.

She wanted to adopt a baby? Sly realized his mouth was hanging open and quickly shut it. "Is that right."

The girl wore a speculative expression. "I changed my mind about leaving," she said. "I might stay a while longer. But I need to use the restroom. Excuse me." She slid out of the booth and hurried away.

"This is awkward," he said in the silence that fell between him and Lana.

"The part about me wanting to adopt, or about me not hearing from you since you stopped at the day care?" Her eyes flashed with anger. "Or do you mean because you're suing my cousin?"

So she and Tim Carpenter *were* related. Sly muttered a choice oath and put his head in his hands. With a look of alarm, Dani approached, quickly filled his cup and left.

"First of all, until this minute I wasn't aware you and Tim Carpenter were related," he said. "I didn't even know your last name until I read it in the paper."

"That's understandable, but you're still suing my cousin."

Her stony expression made him hurry to explain. "Trust me, it wasn't my first choice. Tim didn't leave me any other option." Wanting to get to other things before Sophie returned to the table, Sly added, "I'll tell you about that later. FYI, I wanted to ask for your number before I left you in our hotel room. But we agreed that we wouldn't contact each other again."

"Then why did you come to my day care?"

"I wanted to see you."

"For exactly one reason." Lana glanced around and lowered her voice. "You wanted a repeat of what happened that night."

"True," Sly admitted, "but it wasn't just about sex. I'm not interested in getting serious or anything, but I would like to get to know you."

"Oh, really? Then why didn't you ask me for my number, or at least act like you were interested in *me* as a person? You never asked me a single question about myself."

Sly fiddled with his cup. "You didn't ask me any questions, either."

"I was letting you take the lead!"

People were starting to stare.

Lana lowered her voice. "Forget it."

"Uh, can I have your number now?" Talk about sounding lame.

"It's a little late for that, Sly. Besides, you haven't explained why you filed a lawsuit against my cousin."

"There's a simple—"

"I have to leave after all," Sophie said as she returned to the booth. "While I was in the bathroom, my mom called. She wants me to get home and finish my chores before I leave for work."

Lana nodded and then nudged Sly out of the booth and stood up. "I enjoyed meeting you, Sophie. I hope we'll get together again soon."

"Can I let you know?"

"Sure. I'll walk you out."

"You stay here with Sly." The girl's smile was meant for the two of them.

Sly squelched the urge to roll his eyes. "Nice meeting you." He sat down in Sophie's place so that he would be across from Lana.

"You, too, Sly. Hey, next time Lana and I get together, you should join us."

Sly glanced at Lana, but her attention stayed on the teen.

It was obvious how badly she wanted things to work out between them.

"If I'm not too busy at the ranch," he said.

"I knew you were a rancher!" Sophie turned to Lana. "Thanks for brunch. It was really good."

"Anytime." Lana bit her lip. "Would you mind if I gave you a hug?"

"I guess."

Feeling like he was watching something that was none of his business, Sly stared as Lana embraced the girl.

When she pulled away, her eyes dropped to Sophie's belly. "You take care of that baby, okay?"

"I will."

Her eyes stayed on Sophie until the door closed behind her.

Chapter Five

Angry at Sly for suing her cousin and unhappy at how badly the meeting with Sophie had gone, Lana was ready to leave. "I have a lot to do today," she said, signaling Dani to bring the check. "Enjoy your lunch."

"Stay a little longer and tell me about this baby you want to adopt."

She didn't mind talking about that, but after Sophie's bombshell that she was also meeting with a couple interested in adopting her baby, Lana felt unusually emotional and vulnerable. Just now, she wasn't ready to share anything. But she wouldn't mind some answers from Sly. "I'll stay if you explain about the lawsuit," she said.

"Any minute now, my sister will bring me my burger, and I don't want to ruin my appetite talking about that. I'll give you the details later." Resting his arms on the table, he leaned toward her. "So you want to adopt a baby."

He gave her a long, searching look that made him seem genuinely interested. Lana wanted to explain. If she kept it short and simple, she wouldn't cry. "That's right," she said. "I'm unable to have children myself."

"So you said before. You didn't mention wanting to adopt, though."

"Because we agreed not to get into anything serious."

Besides, they'd been too busy to talk much. "Anyway, now you know."

"If you're sure you want kids, adopting makes sense."

"I'm sure. I've always wanted to be a mom."

Sly nodded, but Lana was curious about the way he'd said *if you're sure you want kids*. "You don't want to have children?" she asked.

"Nope. Don't get me wrong, I like them, as long as they belong to someone else."

"You mean you don't want any right now," she corrected. "My best friend, Kate—you met her that night at the Bitter & Sweet—feels the same way. Kate says she'll be ready when she's thirty-five."

"That's how old I am now, and I mean never. I'd make a lousy father."

"Why do you say that?"

"Trust me, I raised my younger brother, and I know what I'm talking about. Me having a kid would be irresponsible."

"I'd call raising your brother the opposite of irresponsible." Lana was beyond curious now. "Do you mind my asking what happened?"

"It's no secret. I was eleven when my mom died. Two years later, my father also passed away. The child protection people managed to find an uncle who agreed to take in Seth and me. Let's just say our uncle didn't want us around. That's how I ended up raising Seth." Sly shrugged. "That didn't turn out so great."

"What do you mean?"

"For starters, he did a few stupid things that got attention from the law. Uncle George had a problem controlling his temper, so I stepped in. Or I tried." Sly let out a self-derisive laugh. "No matter what I said or what I did, I couldn't get Seth to straighten up or take responsibility for the trouble he caused. Not even moving back to Prosperity helped. Then he dropped out of high school."

That sounded like a tough situation. Lana bit her lip. "Where is Seth now?"

"I have no idea. When he was seventeen, he split. A few weeks later, he sent a postcard to let us know he was okay. He hasn't been in touch since." Sly glanced down at his empty coffee cup, then spread his hands in a gesture of helplessness. "Now you know what a great job I did."

Lana pictured a very young Sly struggling to raise his brother when he was so young himself. "You were under very challenging conditions, Sly. You were an orphan and a child yourself. Under those circumstances, no one would do well."

He was unconvinced. "Because of the situation, I grew up fast. At fourteen, I was more mature than most eighteen-year-olds. I should have done a better job. Instead, I screwed up my brother and also blew any chance of a tight relationship with him."

Lana thought Sly was too hard on himself, and felt terrible for him and his brother. "I'm sorry."

"It was a long time ago. I'm over it now. But I won't ever screw up a kid that way again."

"Isn't Dani your sister? She seems to have turned out well."

"No thanks to me. Our uncle didn't want any girls around, so Dani went into foster care. She was lucky enough to get Big Mama as her foster mom. A couple of years later, Big Mama adopted her. So yeah, I'm all for adoption."

Dani slid Sly's burger and a soda in front of him. "Here's your burger, Sly. Are you telling Lana about my adoption?" After waiting for his nod, Dani went on, "I'm so lucky to have Big Mama as my mom. Even if we *are* both hardheaded." She flashed a truly happy grin. "How about a piece of coconut cream pie, Lana?"

Lana was hungry now, and pie sounded good. But she didn't plan on sitting here long enough to eat it. "No, thanks. I'm leaving in a few minutes," she said. "We're talking about adoption because I'm planning to adopt."

"Is that why you were buying that pregnant teen brunch? I wondered. How exciting!"

"Cross your fingers. Sophie has a meeting with a married couple who also want her baby, and I'm worried she'll choose them."

"Because they're a couple and you're single?" When Lana nodded, Dani scoffed. "Big Mama was a single mom, and she did a super job raising me. Wish I had more time to talk, but as you can see, we're slammed. Sly will give you my number. Call me, and let's get together."

"That'd be great."

Dani smiled and left.

"I really like your sister," Lana said.

"She's good people." Sly took a bite of his burger.

His food smelled great. He caught her staring at his potato chips, which were homemade and out of this world. "Have one."

"I couldn't," Lana said. But she took one anyway. "I really should leave."

"I haven't had a chance to explain about the lawsuit. I get that you're upset about it, but I'd like a chance to give you my side."

Lana wanted to hear it, and Big Mama's chips were impossible to resist. As was Sly. And so she stayed.

DESPITE LANA'S PROTESTS, Sly ordered more chips. He waited to discuss the lawsuit until Dani set a fresh plate on the table and left.

"I first met Tim Carpenter seven years ago, not long after the state reimbursed me for the small ranch I owned. They needed the property to put in a new freeway, and I needed a new ranch. Lucky for me, the Martinson place came on the market. It was bigger than the one I gave up, with a lot of potential. The Martinsons were about to go into foreclosure and asked a fair price, so I bought it."

"Then you've always been a rancher?"

Sly shook his head. "I never made a conscious decision to make ranching a career. When I was in college, I needed a job and found work at a ranch. Ranching is in my blood now, though, and I feel I was born to do it. After I bought the Martinson place, I learned that your cousin had figured on cutting a deal and buying the land dirt cheap. He wasn't happy that I offered the asking price."

"I remember hearing him talk about that at a Fourth of July family barbecue," Lana said.

Unable to imagine a worse man to spend a holiday with, Sly made a face. "That must've been a real fun get-together."

"Cousin Tim isn't the nicest guy, but at holiday gatherings he's usually in a pretty decent mood." Lana paused to munch a chip. She seemed to really like them. "I enjoy hanging out with family," she went on. "If I didn't, I wouldn't have dinner at my parents' house every Sunday. My sister and her husband and kids go, too. Sometimes my mom gets on my nerves—well, okay, a lot of the time—but the kids make it fun."

Sly wondered what it was like to be part of a family that got together for dinner once a week and attended big family barbecues. He had a few memories of his parents grilling, and friends and neighbors coming over for a meal. His family had lived in a pretty little house with a nice yard and a neighborhood filled with families just like theirs.

"The day I moved to Pettit Ranch, I made a point of going over to the Lazy C and meeting Tim," Sly said. "He was never what I'd call friendly, but we nodded when we saw each other. Then three months ago, I lost three cattle. Over the next few days, several more got sick, and two of my pregnant heifers miscarried. A cow will usually bear four to five calves over her lifetime, but those two will never be able to conceive again." The loss of ten calves meant a bundle of lost revenue.

"That's terrible." Lana grimaced. "My mom ran into Cousin Tim a few weeks ago and he mentioned that you'd lost some cattle, but he didn't share the details."

"It sucks, all right. My crew and I had no idea about the poison at first. We tested for all the usual diseases, but the results were negative. The vet couldn't figure out what was wrong. He ordered autopsies. They showed that my animals had been poisoned."

Sly had entered Big Mama's a hungry man. His burger was delicious, but suddenly he couldn't eat another bite.

Lana wasn't going after the chips anymore, either. Her face had paled and she looked shocked. "I've never heard of anything like that before. It's horrific."

Sly agreed. He'd spent more than a few sleepless nights wondering what kind of person would poison an animal, and fearing that even more might sicken and die. The feeling of powerlessness had settled in his chest like a dark weight, just as it had after his father had passed, leaving him and his siblings alone.

"What makes you believe my cousin did it?" Lana asked.

"Long story short, there's a private service road along the north side of my ranch that runs between my land and Tim's. The only people with access to it are me and my crew, and Tim and his. Remember that freakish warm weather in January that melted all the snow? By sheer chance, my foreman was driving a truck of feed down that road and happened to notice a piece of a bag label and a small pile of white powder just inside the fence of one of our pastures. We weren't sure what it was and sent a sample of the powder to a lab. It turned out to be arsenic."

Every time Sly thought about it, a slow burn started in his blood. His fingers tightened into fists.

Lana stared at his hands with wide eyes. "I have no idea what to say."

With effort, he forced his fingers to relax. "Yeah, it's kind of a conversation stopper. Accidents happen, and at first I kept an open mind. You hit a bump, or drive over a pothole, and things can fall off a flatbed without the driver realizing. By some fluke, it could have landed inside the fence.

"None of my men had transported arsenic in their trucks. I decided to ask Tim about it. Hell, he might have had a legitimate reason for buying the stuff. I tried to talk to him twice, but he refused to even discuss the matter. He got downright belligerent, even aimed a gun at me. I figured bringing in someone else might *encourage* him to help clear up a few questions. So I hired an attorney."

Sly shook his head. "Fat lot of good that did. Tim was just as stubborn and closemouthed with him. He's been so ornery and nasty that I can't help but think that he deliberately put that arsenic on my land."

Lana frowned. "But why would he do that?"

Sly had given that a lot of thought. "I wish to hell I knew. To get back at me for buying the ranch? Or maybe because I'm turning a profit and he isn't."

"My cousin can be a real jerk, but I can't imagine him doing something like that."

"I'm sorry it had to be your cousin," Sly said, and he genuinely was.

Lana looked just as sorry. "My family sticks together through thick and thin. Once, when my mother's cousin Millie lost her job at a farm supply store due to cutbacks, the entire family bombarded the owner with calls and letters, asking that he reinstate her. He didn't have the resources to rehire her or any of the other people he laid off. Our family took out an ad in the paper, asking people in Prosperity to please patronize that store to increase business and help the laid-off employees get their jobs back. The ad generated a ton of new business, and eventually the owner was able to rehire cousin Millie and several other former employees."

Sly couldn't imagine having a family so tight. He envied Lana. "That's impressive."

She nodded. "What are you asking for in the lawsuit?"

"An apology and a reimbursement for what the poisoning cost me—thirty thousand dollars."

"That's a lot of money."

"Raising cattle is expensive. The feed, the vaccines and vitamins, the costs of maintaining all that fencing. Plus losing the unborn calves, as well as the future calves of the cows who died and the two who are now sterile—it adds up. The tests and autopsies alone cost me a small fortune. That money was earmarked for a new drainage system." Sly sipped his coffee, which had grown cold. "That's my story."

Lana dipped her head and smoothed her napkin so that her hair swung forward, hiding her expression. She was easy to read when Sly could see her face, and he wished she'd look up or say something more so that he'd have a clue what she was thinking.

Though he was sure it wasn't good.

He cleared his throat. "I should get back to the ranch, and you have things to do."

He left Dani a big tip, and walked out with Lana. As

she moved toward her car, he touched her arm. "I haven't given you Dani's number. I'm sure she'll want yours, too."

Between the lawsuit and the baby she wanted to adopt, exploring their attraction seemed impossible. But Sly lost himself in her beautiful eyes. "So would I," he added.

Lana hesitated, her expression regretful. "I want you to call me, Sly, but even if you do have a legitimate reason for suing my cousin, you aren't sure that he did it. I have to support my family. Goodbye."

She walked away.

LANA WOKE UP Sunday morning thinking about Sly. After their conversation yesterday at Big Mama's, she liked him more than ever. But she was also convinced that they shouldn't see each other again.

As she sipped her morning coffee and read the Sunday paper, sleeting rain battered the windows. The weather was supposed to clear by noon, but the dark gloom suited her mood. This was a perfect day to stay home and work on the nursery. Because Sophie *had* to choose her.

If she didn't... Lana refused to let herself go down that path.

A few hours later, she stood in the nursery and admired the freshly painted walls. The soft yellow color made the formerly chocolate-brown room appear bigger and cheerier. It would look even better when she painted the children's mural next weekend.

After changing out of her paint clothes, Lana headed downstairs, flopped on the sofa and phoned Kate. "How was your blind date last night?" she asked when her friend picked up.

"As bad as I predicted. Henry had slippery hands and bad breath. He took me bowling. I have no problem with that, but on a first date? That's the last time I let my mother set me up with anyone, ever. How was brunch with Sophie?"

"That didn't go so well, either." Lana filled her in. "Then Sly showed up."

"Oh?" Kate sounded intrigued.

"As it turns out, his sister is Big Mama's adopted daughter. Dani's great. You'd like her."

"I know Dani from when I eat there. She's a sweetheart. I even remember she had a brother, but I didn't realize he was Sly. Now, there's a guy I'd want someone fix me up with—if you hadn't snagged him first."

"Snagged him? You're funny. And now…" Lana blew out a heavy breath.

"That's some sigh. Tell me what happened."

"If you'll just be patient, I will."

"Okay, okay. Start from the beginning."

"Sophie was getting restless, but as soon as Sly sat down with us, she totally changed." One smile and she'd been as smitten as Lana. "He pretty much snowed her."

"Well, yeah. He's a gorgeous man. But get out! Sly sat at your table?"

"It was a booth, and he only joined us because all the other tables were taken."

"Really," Kate said in a tone that reminded Lana of a cooing dove. "And how did that go?"

"Pretty well. After Sophie left, we—"

"Sophie left? I thought she liked Sly."

"She did, but she had to get home."

"So she left and you and Sly stayed. In a nice, cozy booth. This is starting to head in the right direction. Go on."

Lana rolled her eyes. "We talked. I explained why I treated Sophie to breakfast. I also learned some interesting things about him." She filled in her friend about Sly's childhood and the lawsuit.

"You two sure made up for lost time in the talking department. I'll bet he finally asked for your number, huh?"

"He did, but I didn't give it to him."

"Are you nuts? Why the heck not?"

"Did you not listen to what I said? Sly is suing my cousin and I'm getting ready to adopt a baby. I can't get involved with him."

"That's just plain crazy. The adoption isn't for months yet, and you can't just stay home, twiddling your thumbs. As for your cousin, you can hardly stand him. The one time I met him, I didn't care much for him, either. If Tim did the crime, he *should* pay."

Lana sighed. "No one can be sure he poisoned those cows, Kate. Refusing to answer Sly's questions doesn't make him guilty."

"But he pointed a *gun* at Sly."

"Yes, but it doesn't prove anything. And don't forget my parents. I want to be able to bring whoever I'm dating to their house for Sunday dinner. If he happens to be suing a member of our family, it just won't work."

"I've met Sly, remember?" Kate said. "Besides being drop-dead gorgeous with a killer smile, he oozes charm. Lawsuit or not, once your parents meet him, they're bound to love him."

"If only it was that easy. Even if Sly charmed them to death, on principle alone they won't accept him."

"It'll be months before you're at the point where you want Sly to meet your parents—maybe long after the lawsuit gets settled," Kate said. "Heck, you two may never even get that far. But you owe it to yourself to find out."

That made sense. "When you put it that way… Now I wish I *had* given him my number."

Lana could picture her friend's big smile.

"Why don't you call him?" Kate suggested. "I'm sure his number's in the phone book."

"Only if he has a landline. I'm not going to do that."

"Then just show up at Big Mama's next Saturday. He'll probably be back. If that doesn't work, ask his sister for his number."

None of Kate's suggestions appealed to Lana. Besides, today she had other things on her mind. She checked her watch. "Sophie's meeting with that couple right now—the Andersons—but I refuse to let it bother me."

"That's the spirit."

"They're a married couple and I'm a single woman," Lana said, anxious despite her bravado. "Sophie said that didn't matter to her, but what if it does? What if she chooses them?"

"You'll drive yourself crazy worrying about that, Lana, so don't. It's obvious to me that you're interested in Sly. He seems interested in you, too, so why not encourage him? I'm not saying you should ask him out, but a phone call can't hurt."

"If I could say for sure that my cousin actually poisoned those cattle, I probably would call Sly. But I can't. My parents would flip out."

"I don't understand you, Lana. You're thirty-two years old. What do you care if they're upset?"

"You're not as close to your mom and dad as I am to mine," Lana explained. "When they're unhappy with me, they make my life miserable. Look at how they're responding to my wanting to adopt."

"Well, then, you'd better forget all about Sly Pettit."

"That's exactly what I'm going to do."

Chapter Six

Sly's truck was running on fumes when he pulled into the gas station Sunday afternoon. He wasn't the only driver in need of fuel, and the only available pump happened to be the one adjacent to where Tim Carpenter was about to fill his truck.

Talk about awkward. "Hey," Sly said with a terse nod.

Carpenter scowled at him. "Don't 'hey' me. You can sue me to hell and back, but it won't change the fact that I didn't do a damn thing to your cattle. I won't apologize for something I didn't do, and I'll die before you get a dime out of me. Stick *that* up your fancy lawyer's butt. Better yet, I'll let my lawyer do that."

His voice had grown steadily louder. People were staring now.

So Carpenter had hired himself an attorney. He needed one. Sly raked his hand through his hair and strove for calmness, but he was seriously pissed. His neighbor's nastiness only made things worse. He shook his head. "Hasn't anyone ever told you that being an ass is a sure way to make your life miserable?"

"You're the ass." Carpenter's fist shot toward Sly's nose.

Sly dodged the punch and caught hold of the man's wrist. "I wouldn't try that again if I were you," he warned in a low voice.

Narrowing his eyes, Carpenter wrenched free and spat on the ground. "I'll get my gas someplace else."

He jumped into his truck and roared off.

Nearby, a man Sly didn't know shook his head. "He's got a temper on him, that one."

Gus Jones, a fellow rancher, left his Jeep at the pump and joined Sly. "Tim Carpenter has never been an easy man to deal with, but that was the worst I've ever seen him. You okay?"

Aside from his near miss with Carpenter's fist and a big adrenaline rush, Sly was fine. He nodded.

After filling the tank and paying, he left. When he got home, he was still so rattled that he jumped bareback on Bee and gave her free rein. Before long they were flying across the ranch, with the wind at their backs and nothing to see but livestock and acres of his rolling fields. Eventually Sly calmed down.

That evening he called and updated Dave Swain. "After the rains we had last weekend, one of the lower pastures flooded," he explained. "I need the money Carpenter cost me for my new drainage system, and I need it now. I want you to add a penalty to the lawsuit, so that every day Carpenter delays the settlement, it costs him more."

"I wouldn't advise that," Dave said. "It'd be like rubbing salt into the wound, and could make things even worse."

Thinking it over, Sly had to agree. "Okay, so now what do we do?"

"Sit tight," Dave said, "and let us lawyers earn our fees."

Sly didn't enjoy playing this particular waiting game. Especially now, during the rainy season. Every day Carpenter delayed put the ranch in more jeopardy.

THE RAINS WERE heavy over the next week, and Sly divided his long days between spring calving and digging new ditches. The old system worked only sporadically now. Though the ditches diverted some of the water and reduced the danger of flooding, copious amounts of mud clogged every low-lying pasture. Cattle got stuck in the stuff. Fortunately, as yet none had fallen or sustained injuries, but they had to be moved. Sly, Bean and Ollie had herded them to higher ground.

Between that and the usual ranching chores, they were all stretched thin. With so much on his plate, Sly barely had a moment to grab a decent meal, let alone think about Lana during the day. But at night when he should have been dead to the world, he lay in bed, wanting her. They were as mismatched as a flip-flop and a cowboy boot, and getting involved with her would only lead to trouble.

Regardless, his desire for her continued to grow, until he had to kiss her again or lose his mind. If he was lucky, he wouldn't enjoy the kiss half as much as he remembered. Then it would be easier to forget about her.

That Saturday he spent a wet morning checking for new calves and looking for signs of heifers in labor. Around noon, the rain stopped. Sly was about to head home and change into dry clothes when he came across a black heifer. She was in labor and lying on her side, pushing hard.

He stayed nearby, not too close, but within reach in case she needed help. Using his phone, he snapped a couple of photos. It was an easy birth, and mama cow did fine by herself. Finally, something to grin about.

"Way to go, you two," he said in a low voice that wouldn't startle them.

His first thought was that Lana would enjoy these photos. Covered in mud, he showered, changed, wolfed down a sandwich and then headed for her place.

She lived in a town-house community that was well

maintained. Flower boxes underscored every window of her two-story place, just as they did at the day care.

Bushes lined both sides of her little yard, some already fat with buds on the verge of blooming. A pot of colorful tulips decorated the little stoop beside the door.

Sly pushed the doorbell. Seconds later, she answered. Wearing jeans and a ragged, paint-smeared sweatshirt, with her hair banana-clipped off her face and a smudge of paint on her cheek, she looked cute.

With that, Sly silently admitted that he was here for more than a few photos. He wanted to kiss Lana and find out if she was as sweet as he remembered.

"Sly," she said, her surprised expression almost comical. "What are you doing here?"

"I want to show you something."

"You obviously know where I live. I'm guessing you also have my number. You couldn't call and give me a heads-up that you were coming?"

He'd figured she'd tell him to stay away. "You asked me not to call," he said. "I thought I'd surprise you."

The couple next door, whom he judged to be about his age, stopped their yard work and stared openly at him.

Lana waved at them, then widened the door. "Come in."

After wiping his boots on a welcome mat that resembled a giant sunflower, Sly stepped into a house that felt warm and welcoming. More flowers filled a vase on the end table in the living room. She obviously had a thing for flowers— and bright colors. The whole place was painted in cheerful colors that couldn't help but lift the spirits.

"Nice place," he said.

"Thanks. I bought it after the divorce and have been fixing it up ever since. Do you want something to drink?"

"I'm fine." He shrugged out of his denim jacket and draped it over a nearby chair.

She angled her head slightly, her expression curious. "What did you want to show me?"

"This morning I came across a heifer giving birth and I snapped a few photos." He pulled out his phone and showed her pictures of the heifer licking her baby and nudging it to stand.

She studied each photo, her lips forming a provocative O that almost did Sly in. "Aww, so sweet."

"I figured you'd want to see them," he said, desire making his voice rough.

Oblivious of his need, she handed him back the phone. "You could have forwarded these to me and saved yourself the trip. You still should, so I can show the kids at the day care."

"I will. I didn't send them because there's another reason I stopped by." He slid the phone into his back pocket. "There's something I forgot to give you last Saturday."

She frowned. "Oh?"

Sly stepped closer and kissed her. For all of a blink she held herself stiff. Then she went up on her toes and wrapped her arms around his neck. She was fine boned and barely reached his shoulders. Yet as small and delicate as she was compared to his big frame, she fit as if she'd been made just for him.

He'd imagined he remembered how good she tasted, but he hadn't realized she tasted quite like this. Sweet and cinnamony and something indefinable. She was intoxicating, and he wanted to kiss her forever. And a lot more.

He urged her lips apart and tangled his tongue with hers. Lana made the sound he remembered from their night together, a mixture of a moan and a sigh that drove him wild.

She wriggled closer. God, he wanted her. Smart or dumb, right or wrong, he definitely wanted to keep doing this, keep seeing her. Sliding his hands down her spine, he cupped her hips, bringing her tight against the part of him that was already rigid with desire.

Suddenly she tensed and pushed her hands against his chest. "Stop, Sly."

Reluctantly, he stepped away.

"What was that for?" she asked, frowning but looking thoroughly kissed and sexy as all get-out.

"I've been wanting to do that since the afternoon at the day care." He ran his finger over her lush pink bottom lip, watching with satisfaction as her mouth opened a fraction and her eyes lost focus. "I'm glad I did."

Though she attempted to hold on to her stern expression, she didn't appear to be sorry, either.

"Dani says you two scheduled a get-together."

"That's right, in a few weeks."

Lana didn't invite him to sit down, and he guessed she was about to ask him to leave. "You probably heard what happened at the gas station last weekend," he said, wanting to talk about it before she kicked him out.

She shook her head. "No."

"Your cousin tried to punch me out."

Her eyebrows arched in surprise. "He didn't."

"Yep." Remembering, Sly scrubbed his hand over his face. "Our lawyers have been going back and forth." He hoped things got resolved and settled quickly, because he needed that money yesterday.

Not wanting to get into that, though, he sniffed the air. "I smell paint." He nodded at the smudge on her cheek. "That's a nice shade of green."

Lana touched the spot. Her cheeks reddened. "Why didn't you tell me there was paint on my face?"

"I had other things on my mind." His gaze dropped to her mouth, and damned if he didn't want to kiss her again.

Swallowing, she glanced away. "I've been working on the spare bedroom, making it into the nursery."

"Would you show it to me?" he asked.

"Sure. Follow me."

LANA SENSED SLY checking her out as she led him upstairs. Her whole body hummed, but then, she'd been humming since he'd pulled her into his arms.

Oh, what a kiss. The man was an expert at kissing. He was also a skilled lover. But Lana wasn't going to think about that. At the top of the stairs, they started down the hall.

"It's bigger up here than it appears from outside," Sly said.

"That's one reason why I bought this place—there's so much space. There are two bedrooms up here and a small sunroom at the end of the hall that I use as a home office."

Sly nodded. "This must be your bedroom," he said as they passed the door.

"Yes." Amy and Sheila had commented that Sly always stayed the night at their places, never his. Was he imagining a night here with her? Her cheeks warmed, and she knew she was blushing. "This is the nursery."

Sly stepped into the room, his eyes on the ocean-themed mural she'd sketched out on the wall. "You never said you were a talented artist."

"I wouldn't exactly call myself talented," she said.

"You are, and this is pretty cool."

"Thanks." Lana admired her work, proud of the friendly sea creatures that were still only half-painted. "It's turning out really well. The other day I found some peel-off decals of whales and porpoises to put on the ceiling, over the crib."

"Cool idea. Whoever ends up here will be one lucky kid."

The words were a balm to Lana's heart. "I hope so. I

really want a child." Feeling suddenly vulnerable, she lowered her gaze to the carpet.

"What's wrong?" When she didn't reply, he tipped up her chin. "Lana?"

His eyes were filled with concern, and her anxieties poured out. "I wish I knew who Sophie was going to choose. I've been trying to get together with her again, but I haven't had any luck. We did talk once, but she prefers to text. She says she still hasn't decided between me and the Andersons."

Lana was scared to death about that. "Say a little prayer that she chooses me."

"Will do. Why don't you invite her over to show her what you're doing here? This nursery could tip the scales in your favor. Plus, she'd get a chance to check out the neighborhood and your house."

"That's not a bad idea."

"I understand how important this to you," Sly said. "Sophie said she wanted to see me again. If it helps, I'll come over when she's here."

"You'd do that for me?" Lana wanted to melt.

He actually blushed. Her heart expanded. She liked him a lot. Too much. "I'm not sure about that, Sly."

"Lana, Lana, what am I gonna do with you?"

He touched her cheek. Fighting the urge to sink against him, she ducked out of his reach. "We can't do this," she said.

"What's between you and me has nothing to do with my lawsuit."

"We both know that it does. But it's more than that. We don't want the same things." Except physically. Lana had never ached for a man the way she did for Sly.

As if he'd read her mind, he laughed softly. "Say what you will. You can't fight chemistry like ours. Look, I'll give you my number. You call if you want me to be here when Sophie comes."

That sounded safe enough. "Okay," she said.

They headed downstairs. Sly jotted down his number and handed it to her. Then he grabbed his jacket and shrugged into it, his shoulders impossibly broad.

"I'll let myself out."

Before she had a chance to reply, he was gone.

MONDAYS WERE ALWAYS hectic at the day care, but today had been crazy busy. Lana had scheduled meetings with four different sets of parents and their kids, all of whom were interested in the day care. If that wasn't enough, Brittany, the full-time employee, had called in sick, leaving Lana and Jasmine, her part-time assistant, to deal with the usual Monday chaos.

Naturally, this was the day the guinea pig escaped. Jayden, a rambunctious four-year-old, had been so intent on catching the frightened animal that he'd wet his pants. And he didn't have a change of clothes. Then Valerie, almost four, had vomited all over herself, which had upset all the kids.

Lana couldn't ever remember being this tired. All she wanted was to go home, put up her feet and relax. Unfortunately, she'd worked on the nursery over the weekend instead of picking up any groceries. It was either live on fast food, which wasn't a bad idea once or twice but not for the entire week, buy groceries or starve. That was how she ended up pushing a cart through Sterling Foods during the dinner hour.

To Lana's surprise, for once the busy grocery store was quiet. With any luck, she'd zip in and zip out, and be home in no time. Eager to get the job done, she wheeled her cart toward the produce at warp speed.

Until she rounded the corner and spotted Sly. Abruptly she stopped. He was loading a huge sack of potatoes into his cart. A clean denim shirt hugged his broad shoulders, faded jeans showcased his long, powerful legs, and those cowboy boots... He looked good. Really good.

Two days ago, he'd kissed her senseless. The sight of him now brought it all back—the feel of his strong arms around her, his solid chest against her breasts, his warm, soft mouth on hers....

Her lips tingled and every nerve in her body began to hum. She was about to move away and find a different aisle when Sly spotted her. A slow smile spread across his face. Her heart tumbled over in her chest.

"Sly...hi." Mustering a smile, she wheeled slowly toward him.

"I was just thinking about you," he said.

He was? "I didn't expect to find you here," Lana said. "I mean, it's the dinner hour, and isn't this a superbusy time of year for ranchers?"

"You wouldn't believe how busy. But my housekeeper's husband sprained his back yesterday, and she's taking a few days off to take care of him. Monday happens to be her grocery day, and a man's got to eat, so here I am." He spread his hands. "She made a list of what to buy—a long list. I didn't have a chance to shop until now."

"I'm usually here on Saturdays," Lana said. "But you know how I spent that."

"I sure do." He was close enough that she could see the silver flecks in his eyes aglow with heat.

Her whole body grew warm. She cleared her throat. "I was talking about the mural. I worked on it Saturday night and all day Sunday until I left for dinner at my parents'."

"Did you finish it?"

"There are a few little touch-ups left, but it's basically

done." She was pleased with the results. "I'm going to call Sophie tonight and invite her over."

"Excellent plan. Call if you need me."

Sly tucked a lock of hair behind her ear, as if it was the most natural thing in the world. As if they were together. The humming in Lana's body increased.

She barely registered his words. She was too lost in his heated gaze, the familiar scent of his spicy aftershave, the warm caress of his fingers.

His eyelids dropped to half-mast and she thought he was going to kiss her. *Yes!*

Her body screamed for her to step into his arms. But voices warned her that a mother and a young child were approaching.

Stepping away from Sly, she snatched a head of lettuce from a nearby display. "I'll, uh, keep you posted," she said as she pivoted the cart and hurried away.

Chapter Seven

"I keep running into your brother," Lana told Dani on Wednesday night. They were sitting at Coffee, Tea + Treats in the heart of downtown, sipping tea and eating pie.

She'd seen him Monday at the grocery, and again yesterday at the post office. Lana had been on her way inside to mail brochures to the parents of several prospective preschoolers. Sly had been on his way out. He'd lingered to chat and tempt her with his smoldering eyes yet again.

"That's interesting," Dani said. "I met my brother for dinner last night, and the sly dog never said a word about it."

"There isn't much to say, except that it's weird that we ran into each other twice in two days. I accused him of stalking me, and he said that he wondered if *I* was stalking *him*."

Lana laughed, but there was nothing funny about her feelings. Each time she saw Sly, the heat simmering between them seemed to grow more intense. Even talking about him made her feel restless. She shifted in her chair.

Dani frowned. "You're fidgety tonight."

"Am I?" Lana forced herself to sit still.

"Prosperity isn't a small town, but sometimes it feels that way," Dani said after pausing to eat her pie. "I run into people I know all the time. What if you and Sly have been doing that for years, but didn't realize because you hadn't met each other yet?"

"It's possible," Lana mused. But Sly was so attractive that she was sure she'd have remembered him. "Let's change the subject. Would you mind if I asked you a few questions about adoption? From the adoptee's point of view."

"Not at all. What do you want to know?"

"What was it like for you to be adopted?"

Deep in thought, Dani was silent a moment. "Losing our mom and then our father when I was so little was rough. I was the baby and the only girl, and my parents and my brothers spoiled me rotten. Then suddenly everyone I loved was gone. I hated being separated from my brothers, but as minors, none of us had a say in what happened. I was so happy when Sly and Seth returned home to find me."

"But Seth left again when he was seventeen, right?"

Suddenly somber, Dani nodded. "He dropped out of high school, jotted a goodbye note and just took off."

For a moment, she stared into space at something only she could see. "Neither Sly nor I has heard from him in ages, but not for lack of trying. The postcard came from California, but we never knew exactly where. He could be anyplace." Her shoulders slumped and she let out a heavy sigh. "Seth has washed his hands of both of us, and I'm not even sure why."

Lana couldn't imagine having a sibling who refused to stay in touch. "That must be hard for you."

Dani nodded. "I try not to think about it." She fiddled with her fork. "Back to the adoption. I was six when I went into foster care. It was a relief to have a place to go. Big Mama was a good foster mom, but what I really wanted was a real mother. It turned out she'd always wanted a daughter, so ours was a match made in heaven. By the time I was eight, I had my 'real' mother." No traces of solemnity now. "Not that it's always been roses. Big Mama likes to do things her way, and I prefer my own way. We butt heads a lot, but I know she loves me. And I adore her."

Lana's heart ached with the need to share the same deep love with her own child. "Did Sly mention that I'm converting my guest bedroom into a nursery?" The night before, she'd put the final touches on the mural. "Now all I'm waiting for is the crib and changing table to arrive. Once I put them together, I'll be ready for a baby."

"That sounds exciting."

"It is. Thanks for not lecturing me about jumping the gun and spending all my spare time and some of my savings when I'm not even sure I'll get this baby."

"Who would put you on such a downer?" Dani asked.

"My mother. She's against what I'm doing. Not adoption per se, but adopting as a single mom. She believes running my own business takes up way too much time for me to raise a child, especially when I'm on my own."

"Hey, if Big Mama raised me and managed her restaurant successfully, I don't see why you can't do the same thing."

"Exactly. I painted a mural on the wall, and it turned out well. I'm hoping that if Sophie comes over I can impress her with it. I so want her to pick me to adopt her baby."

"Inviting her over—that's a great idea."

Lana nodded. "Credit Sly for that. After he saw the mural I was painting, he—"

"Hold on. My brother has been to your *house?*"

"Last Saturday, and he didn't stay long."

Just long enough to make her head spin.

Dani's eyebrows lifted. "It's not like him to just drop by without calling first. What's wrong with that man?"

"I asked him not to call, and I guess he listened." Lana

could count on one hand the number of men who'd really listened to her in her life. Her father, the minister when she'd needed counseling after Brent had left, a single dad or two at the day care who asked for advice about their kids. And Sly.

The more time she spent with him, the luckier she counted herself. He was considerate and warm, he listened and he kissed like a dream. She was sorry the lawsuit prevented her from getting to know him better.

"That day at Big Mama's, he really impressed Sophie," she said. "When she mentioned something about wanting to see him again, he offered to come over if—no, *when*—she visits."

"Sly did that? He's superbusy at the ranch right now, so that's pretty amazing. Have I mentioned what a great guy my brother is?"

"Oh, once or twice." Lana laughed.

But Dani wasn't smiling, she was dead serious. "Are you interested in him?"

"After my divorce, I'm still a little gun-shy. Besides, right now, I'm focusing on the adoption."

"So? Sophie isn't due for months yet and you can't just sit around, waiting. Occasionally, you have to go out and have a little fun. Sly is fun. But you danced with him, so you're already aware of that."

He was more than fun, a lot more. But Lana wasn't going to share that with his sister. "He has a bit of a reputation."

"You've heard about that, have you?" Dani wrinkled her nose. "It's true, my brother used to be quite the ladies' man. Not so much anymore."

"Did he have a bad breakup?" Lana asked. Sly hadn't brought up any past romances, but then, she'd never asked.

"Is a breakup ever good? Mine never are. Years ago, Sly had a serious girlfriend, and last year he dated someone for a while. But as always, things didn't work out." Dani shrugged. "As the queen breaker-upper and breakup-ee, I understand the process only too well. But eventually you have to move on. I mean, I always do."

She sounded just like Kate. "Sometimes healing the heart takes a while," Lana said. "It did for me."

"I'm sure Sly isn't carrying a torch for any of his exes. But he hasn't dated much since his last breakup. That's why, when he mentioned you, I got excited. Now that I know you, I'm doubly thrilled."

"I think you're great, too," Lana said. "But don't expect anything to happen with Sly and me. Besides the adoption and his reputation, he's suing my cousin."

"There is that. But the lawsuit is tearing him up. Sly has never sued anyone before. He wouldn't be doing it now unless he had to. When I heard what happened at the gas station last week…"

"It sounded horrible." Lana closed her eyes a moment and shook her head.

Her cousin claimed that Sly had provoked him, but several bystanders corroborated Sly's version of the incident. If only the two men would settle their differences…

Glum, she rested her chin heavily on her fist. "I'm not sure what to think about any of it. I wish just they'd sit down and work things out."

Then, if she wanted to date Sly—and despite all the reasons why that wasn't a good idea, she did—she could do so without feeling as if she were betraying her family. She'd also have to somehow make sure that dating him wouldn't impact any possible adoptions. Of course, if Sophie chose her, Sly would pose no problem. But the jury was still out on that.

"They could definitely work it out if your cousin would pay up and apologize."

"But what if he isn't responsible for what happened?" Lana asked.

"Then…I have no idea." Dani tightened her ponytail. "Trust me, Sly has tried to talk with him several times. The way he's acted makes him look guilty."

"Cousin Tim can be a real jerk, all right," Lana agreed. "But he's family, and I have to support him."

Her parents ought to give her decision to adopt the same unflagging support, she thought. Next time they gave her grief, she'd point that out to them.

"I guess so, but it makes me sad. Maybe this poisoned-cattle thing will sort itself out. I hope so, because you and Sly would make a great couple. If you give this thing between you a chance, you might even have a shot together. Promise me you won't write him off."

"I promise," Lana said, wondering at herself. For so many reasons, she and Sly were wrong for each other.

Weren't they?

But her promise was enough to make Dani's face brighten. "Regardless of what happens between you and my brother, we can still be friends, right?"

Lana smiled. "Absolutely. What about you, Dani? Are you dating anyone?"

"A guy named Paul, but it's not serious. He's not exactly the man of my dreams, but he's cute and sexy. Unfortunately, he has a bad habit of not showing up when he says he will, and he's canceled dates at the last minute." Dani sighed. "But I like him, so I put up with it. Sly says I have rotten taste in men. He's right, but I can't help who I'm attracted to."

Just as Lana couldn't help being attracted to Sly. "I understand," she said. "By the way, my best friend, Kate Adams, says she knows you."

"Kate's great! She comes into Big Mama's now and

again. Tell her I say hi." Dani glanced at her watch. "Whoa, it's almost nine. I'm due at Big Mama's at five tomorrow morning, so I'd best go home and get some sleep."

"Ugh, that's early."

"We open at six, and someone has to be there. Heck, I'm used to it. And don't forget, we close at four. That means I'm usually out of there by five-thirty, which frees up my whole evening."

Before they parted, they shared a warm hug.

"Let's get together again soon," Lana's new friend said. "Maybe Kate will join us."

Lana smiled. "It's a date."

AFTER A DAY that had started at dawn and finished some twelve hours later, Sly sprawled gratefully on his La-Z-Boy, relieved for some R & R at last. The only things he was good for tonight were sipping a cool one and watching a basketball game. Halfway through the first quarter and his beer, his eyelids dropped shut. He was heading off to la-la land when the trill of his cell phone jerked him awake. Ace and the rest of the crew would call if anything went wrong, but right now, an emergency was the last thing Sly wanted to deal with. Grumbling, he slid the phone from his hip pocket.

Lana Carpenter, the screen said. His sister had programmed her number into his phone. Well, well. Suddenly wide-awake, he muted the TV and answered, "Hey."

"Hi." She sounded a little breathy and unsure of herself. "Am I calling too late?"

He wasn't about to explain that he'd dozed off. "Nope, I'm sitting here, relaxing." He was also alert now—every part of him. "You must have talked to Sophie," he said.

"We just hung up, and guess what? She's coming over to see the nursery on Saturday!" She made a *squee* sound.

Sly imagined the sparkle in her green eyes and the excited flush on her cheeks. "That's great," he said with a grin.

"Isn't it? And she does want you to be there, if you wouldn't mind." She rushed on. "Coincidentally, the furniture store in the mall called this afternoon. The rocking chair, baby lamp, crib and changing table I ordered will be delivered to me tomorrow. I'll have to assemble the crib and changing table, but I can take care of that tomorrow night. When Sophie arrives, the nursery will be perfect."

"Putting furniture together can be tricky. If you need help, I'm your man."

Her man? Had he really just said that? Then again, it was just a figure of speech.

"Thanks, but I'll have the whole evening to tackle the job. It'll be fun."

Some women would jump all over his offer. Not Lana. She was every bit as independent as Dani. Sly admired that. He liked Lana, a lot. Only the more reason to stay away.

"What time should I be there on Saturday, then?" he asked, half regretting his offer to come over. Their kisses the other day had only strengthened his feelings for her. They scared him. It was safer to steer clear of her.

"Shoot, I just realized that I offered to feed Sophie lunch," she mumbled as if to herself. "I'll have to run to the grocery on my way home from work tomorrow night. You're invited to eat with us—if it's possible for you to leave the ranch in the middle of your Saturday."

Her tone had grown muted, as if she expected him to back out. This Saturday happened to be his day to work, but he wasn't about to renege. And not only because he was a man who kept his word.

Lana needed him, and he wasn't about to let her down. He would talk with Ace tomorrow. Knowing the foremen, Ace wouldn't mind if they traded Saturdays.

"I'll make time," he said. "Barring emergencies, I'll stay for as long as you need me." But he'd keep his distance from Lana, and when Sophie left, he'd go, too. That would work.

"Can you come a little before noon?"

Sly nodded, but Lana couldn't see him. "I'll be there."

Chapter Eight

Sophie's text came in just after eight o'clock Friday night. Have 2 postpone 1 week. K?

Lana glanced at the parts of the crib scattered across the rug—screws and springs and things she had no idea what to do with. She'd been struggling to make sense of it all for what seemed like hours and wanted to cry. What kind of idiots had written these stupid assembly directions anyway?

Suddenly she *was* crying. Over impossible instructions and a silly one-week delay. Lately she'd been so emotional, a combination of nerves and PMS.

Sniffling, she replied to Sophie's text. Okay. See you a week from tomorrow at my house.

4 sure, Sophie responded.

Lana needed a break and a glass of wine. No, not wine. Since her big hangover the night she'd met Sly, she'd lost her taste for alcohol. Hot chocolate, then, because she wanted something warm, sweet and comforting. But hot chocolate reminded her of the day she and Sophie had each ordered a mug at Big Mama's. A day that had not gone especially well.

Great, now she was crying again.

Clutching her cell phone, Lana left the mess in the nursery and headed for her bedroom. She flopped on the bed. She wasn't in the best shape to make a call right now, but she had to talk to someone. Kate was going out with friends tonight, but it was early yet. Maybe she was still at home, getting ready. When her friend's voice mail clicked on, Lana disconnected.

Her next thought was to call Sly. He should know about the change in plans. She'd keep the call short, then hang up. His phone rang four times, and Lana guessed that he was probably out, too. Maybe on a date.

Her disappointment was almost as keen as it had been when she'd read Sophie's text. Lana didn't understand herself at all. Just because she was stuck at home didn't mean Sly should be. The man had a right to go out. She was gearing herself up to leave a cheerful-sounding voice message when he picked up.

"Hey, Lana," he said. His low, intimate tone vibrated through her.

Her heart let out a sigh of relief, and suddenly she felt much better. She sat up and propped herself up against the pillows and the headboard. "Hi. How are you?"

"Not bad. This has been a day and a half crammed into about nine hours. I spent most of it separating the yearling heifers from the rest of the herd and inoculating them with hormones to more or less synchronize their heat cycles."

"Why in the world would you do that?"

"So that we can artificially inseminate all of them at once—if they all synchronize, that is. It takes longer for some heifers to reach that point of their cycle."

"That sounds…interesting."

"Trust me, it sounds better than it is."

Hearing Sly's deep chuckle, Lana couldn't help but smile.

"Did you get the crib and stuff put together?" he asked.

Her smile faded. "No. It's a lot harder than I thought." Darn it, the tears were back, blurring her vision and clogging her throat. "Sophie postponed until next week," she said, her voice thick with disappointment.

"You're crying."

"No, I'm not," she said, an involuntary sob escaping. "I'm just so frustrated!"

"Because Sophie changed her plans or because you're having trouble with the furniture?"

"Both!"

Sly was quiet a moment. "She said she'll be over next Saturday, so what's the problem? You worry too much."

He was right. Lana blew her nose.

"In a way, this is good news," he added. "Now you have more time to put the furniture together and get ready for her visit."

"That's true. Thanks for putting a positive spin on this. I feel silly for crying."

"Dani does it, too, once in a while. It's a girl thing."

Lana snorted. "Guys cry, too."

"Nah, we go out and chop wood or run after stray cattle. You'd be surprised how chasing a cow into a glen and out again makes a man forget his problems. Especially when the unexpected happens. Just this morning, Ollie, a kid who works for me, helped me with a renegade heifer. On my way down the glen, I slipped on a fresh cow patty and landed on my as—butt. Ollie almost wet himself, he laughed so hard."

Picturing that, Lana laughed, too.

"And here I'd hoped you'd feel my pain."

That was even funnier. "Thanks, Sly."

"For what?"

"Making me laugh."

She could almost feel his warm smile through the phone.

"Hey, why don't I come over tonight and help you with the furniture?" he said.

It was pathetic how badly she wanted his company. She

bit her lip. "I don't want to ruin your Friday-night plans. In case you're going out."

"I don't have any plans. I'll be over in half an hour."

While Lana waited for Sly, she washed her face, fixed her hair and makeup and exchanged her sweats for a blouse and jeans. She even brushed her teeth.

"Why am I doing this?" she asked her reflection. Of course, it didn't answer.

She was making popcorn when Sly knocked on the door. He wiped his feet and entered her house. He wore a pressed shirt and jeans. His short hair was damp, and he smelled fresh and clean, as if he'd showered before coming over.

They were both dressed as if this were a date. It wasn't. Lana couldn't date a man who didn't want kids and who was suing her cousin. Sly was here to help with the furniture, that was all.

If only she could stop the flutter of excitement in her stomach.

"Thanks for coming over," she said. "I really appreciate it."

"No problem." He sniffed the air. "Do I smell popcorn?"

She nodded. "I figured I should at least feed you something while we work. Would you like a beer to go with it?"

"How did you guess?" Sly said on the way to the kitchen.

He'd only been here once, and already he seemed comfortable in her house. Lana pulled a cold beer from the refrigerator. "My dad always says that popcorn and cold beer go together as well as shoes go with socks."

"Smart man."

"He is. You'd like him." He would probably like Sly, too, but thanks to the lawsuit, they would undoubtedly never meet.

She handed Sly the bottle opener and reached in the cabinet for a glass.

"Don't bother. I prefer it straight from the bottle." He frowned. "You're not joining me?"

Lana shook her head. "I haven't had alcohol since the night we, um, met. Just haven't wanted it. That hangover did me in. Tonight I'm a soda girl, and I prefer mine in a glass. I'll bring the popcorn and some hand wipes if you'll grab the drinks."

They headed up the stairs.

In the nursery, Sly set the drinks on the dresser, the only piece of furniture besides the rocking chair and lamp that didn't require assembly. He took in the mess on the floor. "You've been hard at it."

"Without much success, as you'll notice. The directions may as well be written in Chinese. They're impossible to understand."

"Those things usually are pretty useless." Sly's mouth quirked. "I study the picture, and then figure it out."

"I'm not mechanically minded. I never have been, and I hate that."

"You can't be good at everything. You're an artist and you sure are great with kids."

"How would you know? You've never seen me with kids."

"I just do. And I read that article."

After shoving a handful of popcorn into his mouth, he hunkered down and set to work. He rolled up his sleeves to the middle of his forearms. Lana couldn't help noting his thick wrists and hands.

The nails were short and clean, and his fingers and palms were callused and scarred from ranch work. Strong, competent hands that could also be gentle and bring such pleasure....

She went warm all over before she firmly pushed her desire away and joined him on the floor. "What can I do?"

"For starters, hand me that small, open-ended wrench."

With Sly seeming to understand what went where and in what order, the job wasn't nearly as intimidating.

An hour later the drinks and popcorn were gone, and the crib and changing table were in their places near the mural.

"You saved me hours of bashing my head against the wall," Lana said. "Now all that's left is sewing the curtains, hanging a few pictures and making up the crib."

"This room is welcoming and friendly. Hell, so is your whole house. If I were a kid, I'd sure want to live here."

Lana soaked up the compliment like a dry sponge in warm water. "I just hope Sophie shares your view."

"It's a sure bet she will."

"But is this enough for her to select me as the mom for her baby?" Lana couldn't even fake a cheerful smile.

"You look like you could use a hug."

Sly opened his arms. As soon as she walked into his embrace, he pulled her close, wrapping her in his warmth.

Lana couldn't imagine a place she'd rather be. Her worries melted away, and she was glad she'd promised Dani she wouldn't write off Sly. She could get used to this. He'd been so supportive of her problems with Sophie and her longing to adopt. Maybe she'd misunderstood him. Maybe he wanted kids after all.

They could talk about that later. With a sigh, she snuggled closer. "You give great hugs."

He made a sound of pure male pleasure. "You're easy to hug."

For a few delicious moments neither of them moved. Lana's heart pounded. Sly shifted closer and her whole body began to hum.

He tipped up her chin with his big, warm hand. "Hey, Lana?"

"What?"

His thumb traced her bottom lip. The silver flecks in his eyes seemed to recede, making his eyes bluer and darker. "This." He kissed her.

FORGETTING THAT HE'D vowed to keep his distance from Lana and half waiting for her to stop him, Sly brushed his mouth lightly against hers. She surprised him by wrapping her arms around his neck and pulling him in for a deeper kiss. One kiss became another, and another. She tasted of popcorn and soda and woman.

That was his last coherent thought. Already hard, he sank to the carpet and brought her with him onto his lap. Her soft behind pressed against his erection. She wriggled closer—heaven and hell. On the verge of losing control, he gripped her hips and forced her to be still. "Easy," he said.

She nipped his lower lip, licked it and shimmied her tongue around his mouth. His tenuous grasp on self-control frayed and snapped.

Keeping his mouth fused with hers, Sly undid the tiny buttons on her blouse, almost ripping them off in his haste.

Lana was making the impatient noises he remembered from their night together, little breathy sounds, urging him to hurry. She was driving him wild.

Finally she pushed his hands away and finished the job herself. Her blouse fell open. Her gaze locked on Sly as she slipped out of it.

With hands that trembled, he traced the pink lace edging her bra. Her nipples stiffened, and he hadn't even touched her breasts yet. She was so responsive, the most passionate woman he'd ever met. He slid his fingers inside her cups. Her skin was soft and warm and she smelled sweet and tempting, a mixture of gardenia perfume and her own woman scent. His fingers slid to her nipples.

She inhaled sharply. It wasn't an aroused sound, but a painful gasp.

Sly pulled his hands away. "I'm hurting you."

She shook her head. "My breasts are a little tender, but they get this way before my period."

"Should I stop?"

Instead of answering, she shook her head again, silently covered his hands with hers and guided them to where they'd been.

With a groan, he kissed her again and again, until he was desperate to touch her.

Mindful of her sensitivity, he slowly and lightly drew his finger across her nipples. "Is this okay?"

"Very okay." Her head lolled to the side and her eyes closed.

He unfastened the bra and removed it. Her breasts were full and heavy and her skin was flushed with arousal.

"I want you," he said, yanking at the buttons on his own shirt. He shed it and gently pushed Lana onto the rug on her back. Half lying on top of her, he ran his tongue over one nipple, then the other, until she was writhing and moaning with desire.

Eager to heighten the pleasure, he slid his hand down her smooth stomach toward the button on her jeans.

Suddenly she tensed and pulled her mouth from his. "*Now* I want you to stop."

What the...? Confused and breathing hard, he sat up. Lana joined him, modestly crossing her arms over the breasts he'd just caressed and loved with his mouth. When seconds ago, she'd acted as if she couldn't get enough and desperately wanted more.

Giving his head a mental shake, Sly retrieved her blouse and bra and handed them to her. "What just happened here?"

Ignoring the bra, Lana put on her shirt and buttoned it. It wasn't see-through, but knowing she was braless under there wasn't helping him calm down.

"What we were doing—it isn't what I want," she said.

"Could have fooled me." He picked up his shirt and shrugged into it.

"It wasn't my intention to be a tease, Sly, but when I'm with you…" She glanced down to button her blouse. "I can't help myself."

Now he was doubly confused. "We're attracted to each other and we've already proved how great we are together. What's wrong with enjoying that?"

"As I explained before, I'm not wired for a sex-only thing, Sly. First, I need a deeper relationship."

There it was, the R word, his signal to cut and run.

"So where do we go from here?" he said, surprising himself. He sure as hell wasn't ready to get serious or make any kind of commitment to Lana.

"I'd be more comfortable talking about this in the kitchen."

"Fine by me." He could use a moment to pull himself together.

Trying to ignore the bra that lay on the floor, he set his empty bottle and Lana's glass in the popcorn bowl and followed her down the stairs.

Chapter Nine

Lana's kitchen was about a third the size of Sly's, but homey. He especially liked the breakfast nook that faced the little backyard. The colorful curtains currently drawn against the night gave the space a cozy feel.

"Do you want another beer?" she asked.

"Sure. I'll help myself. How about you—can I get you a fresh soda?"

"You gave up your Friday night to help me out—I'll get you a beer. Please, sit." She gestured toward the nook. "I'm going to switch to herbal tea."

Sipping his beer, he watched her gather the tea fixings. She was facing the stove with her back to him, and he took advantage of the opportunity to look his fill.

Her hair, which hung almost to her shoulders, was every which way, as if she'd just had sex. Her blouse didn't cover her hips or the sweet curve of her behind. When she pivoted around to fill a mug with steaming water, he noticed the points of her nipples poking the blouse.

Sly swallowed hard. *Hard* being the operative word. He wanted Lana more than he'd ever desired a woman. He fantasized about making love with her constantly, and it was killing him. It must be lust that had him sitting at her table, because he sure as hell didn't want a real relationship with her.

At last she brought her tea to the nook and sat down across from him. "Now I'm ready," she said.

Sly sucked in a breath and braced for the dreaded talk.

"I think we should get to know each other without having sex," Lana said.

She meant dating. He could do that and had, lots of times. No big. He let his breath out. "So you're okay about dating now? You said we couldn't because of the situation with your cousin."

"I don't want to discuss him right now." Eyes closed, she rubbed the space between her brows as if the subject gave her a headache.

"You don't like him much, do you?" She didn't reply, and he went on, "It's not as if we're talking anything serious, Lana. It's just dating."

"Are you kidding? If I started going out with you, even casually, my parents would freak out."

Now they were getting somewhere. "Dating isn't necessarily long-term, and it sure doesn't mean getting serious," he repeated.

"All the same, they'd freak out."

"You're scared of them," he suggested, marveling that a grown woman would feel like that.

"That's not it at all. We're a close-knit family. It's easier if we get along."

"Yeah, but that doesn't explain why you're afraid of them."

"I'm not!" Her chin tilted up defensively. "You don't understand what it's like. Let me give you an example. It's been weeks since I told them about my plans to adopt. My mom keeps pressuring me not to do it. She's driving me crazy."

"Tell her to stop."

Lana rolled her eyes. "Like that'd work."

Now he understood. "You're saying that if we're seeing each other, even casually, your mom and dad will give you grief."

"Big-time, and we both know why."

And they were back to the lawsuit. Sly took a long pull of his beer and Lana sipped her tea, the silence between them heavy. They seemed to be circling each other like wagons around a roaring fire.

Returning to a life without Lana was probably for the best, and using her family as a reason to forget each other provided a way out of what could easily become something with strings attached. Sly didn't want strings, but he wasn't ready to let go, either. She was the first woman who hadn't tried to change him, she'd only tried to understand him.

"We don't have to date to get to know one another," Lana said.

Totally confused now, he eyed her warily. "How do we do 'get to know each other' if we don't go out?"

"Hmm."

As she considered the question, the tip of her tongue poked out of the corner of her mouth, which was both tempting and cute.

"We could get together as friends," she finally said.

"Friends," he repeated. Dani had a friend like that, a rancher named Nick Kelly she often hung out with. Nick was an okay guy. Their relationship was platonic. As far as Sly was aware, they'd never even kissed each other. He couldn't ever imagine a platonic relationship with Lana.

"There's too much heat between us to settle for friendship."

To make the point, he leaned across the table and ran the pad of his thumb across her cheek. Instantly her eyes softened and those tempting lips parted a fraction. Sly drew away and dropped his hand. "With one little touch, I just proved that."

"Back to the drawing board." Lana let out a frustrated sigh. "Above all else, I want a child. I hope and pray that Sophie chooses me to adopt her baby. Even if she doesn't…" For a moment Lana's face clouded. "If she doesn't, then I'll keep trying until I finally have the baby I long for.

"I want you to be honest with me, Sly." She pinned him with her big green eyes. "Do you want a relationship with me?"

He wasn't about to lie. "I'm not great at relationships—not the long-term kind," he said. "The truth is, I pretty much suck at them—just ask my last girlfriend."

"I heard plenty from Amy Watkins and Sheila Sommers."

"You talked to Sheila, as well?" He winced.

Lana nodded. "Her son is also enrolled at the day care."

God only knew what the two women had said about him. "Then you get how bad I am at serious relationship stuff." He shook his head. "Why can't we just explore whatever this thing is between us and let whatever happens happen?"

She looked at him funny. "That's exactly what two people do when they have a relationship."

"See, I call that 'casual dating.' The R word sounds way too serious."

"I'm not asking you to fall in love with me, Sly. I'm thinking ahead, to when I adopt."

That could be a long way off yet. By the time it happened, they might not even be interested in each other anymore. "A baby's a big deal," he said cautiously.

"Huge."

"Having a child will change a lot of things in your life."

"In ways I can't even imagine, though believe me, I dream about it constantly." Lana smiled to herself as if she couldn't wait. Then she sobered. "You and I talked about kids once before, and you said you don't want any of your own. But putting the lawsuit aside, can you picture yourself in a stable relationship with me and my child?"

As badly as Sly wanted Lana, getting tangled up with her and her adopted baby scared him. "No," he said.

"That's a deal breaker." She let out a sad sigh. "I guess we won't be seeing each other anymore."

As bad as Sly felt, he had to agree. The thing was, she really wanted the arrangement with Sophie to work, and he wanted that for her. "I'll still come over and help with Sophie next Saturday," he offered.

"I'd appreciate that. I'll make lunch for the three of us."

Sly nodded. "I'll call you next week to confirm the time."

"Okay." She stood up, signaling that the evening had come to an end.

At her door, Sly lingered on the threshold. He started to reach for her, but he'd forfeited the chance to kiss her.

Tipping an imaginary hat, he walked out.

"I CAN'T MAKE it to dinner tonight," Lana told her mother on the phone Sunday. It was almost noon and she was still in bed. "I have the flu."

"You poor thing. Are you throwing up?"

"Twice so far." First at dawn, when nausea had awakened her. She'd barely made it to the bathroom. It had happened again several hours later. She was still weak and nauseous.

"Have you eaten or drunk anything?"

"I'm afraid to."

"You don't want to get dehydrated. Try ginger ale or cola, something easy on the digestive system. If that stays down, nibble a soda cracker and see how that goes."

"Thanks, Mom. I will." If she could just get out of bed without heaving. "There's a flu bug going around the day care. I must've caught it from the kids."

She hoped Sly didn't get it. After those melting kisses… But Lana wasn't about to spend any time dreaming about that. Except for Sophie's upcoming visit, she and Sly weren't going to see each other again.

Which was for the best, but depressing all the same. She'd miss him.

"It isn't the first time," her mother said. Lana had to stop and remember what they were talking about. "Those children bring in all kinds of diseases."

Ah, they'd been talking about getting the flu from her day-care kids.

"Why don't I make you a batch of that chicken vegetable soup you love and bring it over?" her mother went on. "For later, when your stomach settles."

This was her mother at her best—jumping in to help a family member in need. Why couldn't she be this caring and supportive all the time?

As appreciative as Lana was of her mother's solicitude, right now she couldn't even contemplate food, let alone entertain. "That's sweet, Mom, but you really shouldn't. I'll be terrible company, and I don't want you to catch this nasty bug."

"I won't stay long. I'll just pop in, say a quick 'hi' and set the soup and a couple bottles of cola in the fridge for you. They'll keep you hydrated."

"Thanks, Mom." Lana yawned. "I'm going back to sleep now, so that I can get over this thing by tomorrow."

"It wouldn't hurt you to call in sick once in a while. You have two very capable assistants who I'm sure could run the day care just fine without you."

"Jasmine and Brittany are great, but I love going to work."

"Stubborn as always," her mother said. "I'll be over in an hour or so, honey."

MONDAY MORNING, LANA was still queasy, but not sick enough to stay home. She was standing in front of a cupboard at Tender Loving Daycare, choosing supplies for the Monday art project and handing them to her assistants to arrange on the tables, when Jasmine frowned. "No offense, Lana, but you're really pale. You don't look so good."

"You should have seen me yesterday," she said. "You know that flu bug that's going around? I caught it with a vengeance."

Jasmine, who worked mornings and spent her afternoons at the local community college, where she was majoring in early child development, made a face. "Gosh, I hope I don't get it, not with finals coming up."

"Me, either," Brittany said as she placed crayons in trays around the tables. She worked full-time. "I'm saving up for a new car and can't afford to miss work."

They were both in their early twenties and full of energy. They also loved kids. Lana counted herself lucky to have been able to hire them.

"I don't have any classes today," Jasmine said. "I was planning to start writing a paper for my child psych class, but if you need to go home, Lana, I can stay all day."

Lana shook her head. "I appreciate that, Jas, but I'll be okay. I'm a lot better than I was."

The words turned out to be true. By the end of the day, Lana felt her usual self. Tuesday was the same, with a few queasy moments that soon passed. She'd finally kicked the flu bug.

Wednesday morning, Brittany and Jasmine set out the instruments for the weekly music class, which was always fun. Lana was sitting at the desk in the corner, sipping herbal tea and leafing through several well-worn children's books for afternoon story time, when Brittany stilled and made a face. "Uh-oh."

"Please don't tell me you're coming down with the flu," Lana said.

"No, it's my period. I'm a few days early, and I don't have any supplies with me. Help!"

"I keep extras in my locker," Jasmine said. "Come with me."

The two women headed for the employee kitchen on the other side of the day care.

While they were gone, Lana contemplated her own cycle. Between meeting Sly and Sophie, so many things had happened over the past month that she'd barely thought about it. She counted back to her last period—it had finished at the end of March. She should have had another twenty-eight days later, near the end of April.

And here it was, the first week of May, and nothing.

She was never late, never. Was it stress? Maybe, but even during the divorce, which had dragged out for a few months and was exceptionally stressful, her cycle had remained as regular as clockwork.

The implications boggled her mind. Dear God, what if she was truly sick?

Lana sank onto one of the preschool chairs and sought to reassure herself. Aside from the flu, she felt decent enough—except for a queasy stomach in the mornings and at some points during the day. Her breasts were sore, and she'd been more emotional than usual. Even more than when she was PMSing.

Those were all signs of pregnancy.

She couldn't possibly be pregnant. Could she?

The doctor had stated that her chances of getting pregnant were slim to none, which was why she and Sly had skipped using condoms.

Slim to none. That meant there was a teensy bit of a chance.

"Look at you, sitting in one of those little chairs and pale as the butcher-block paper we laid out," Brittany said. "Don't you want to go home?"

Lana managed a fleeting smile. "No, but I think I'd better. Are you two sure you can handle this?"

"I've worked here for almost a year," Brittany said. "And Jas has been here since September. We have the day-care routine figured out."

Lana nodded. "Okay, but if anything happens, be sure to call."

"We will," Jasmine assured her. "Just rest up and get well."

LANA DROVE STRAIGHT to the drugstore. Not quite ready to head inside and buy what she needed, she sat in the car and speed-dialed Kate, who was at work. "Can you talk?" she said.

"I haven't opened the doors yet, so now is good," Kate replied. "Shouldn't you be greeting the first kids of the day about now?"

"I left work."

"You're still sick with the flu. I'm sorry, sweetie. You've got a real nasty bug."

"It's not the flu," Lana said. "I— This is strictly confidential."

"Oh, God, don't tell me it's something even worse."

"Actually, it's wonderful." And scary.

"You've got me really curious. Let me guess—you're sneaking away to meet Sly. Now there's a yummy idea."

"I told you over the weekend that after Sophie comes over this Saturday we decided not to see each other again."

"So? You can still sleep together."

"Will you please stop?" Lana said.

"You don't have to yell." Kate finally got quiet.

Even though Lana was sitting in her car with all the windows up, she lowered her voice to a whisper. "My period is late."

"I can barely hear you. It sounded like you said your period is late."

"You heard right."

"But you're always as regular as clockwork…. Wait just a hot damn minute. Are you saying what I think you are?"

Lana pictured her friend, face aglow with excitement. For the first time since she'd realized that she might be pregnant, she smiled. "I'm sitting in the drugstore parking lot, about to pick up a couple of pregnancy tests. Will you come over after work and keep me company while I take them?"

Kate didn't even pause before answering, "Definitely."

Chapter Ten

It'd been a long day, but to Sly's relief, it hadn't rained. The weather experts predicted a long dry spell. Which was bad for crops, but good for Sly. No more mud for a while. Now would be perfect to install that new drainage system—if he only had the funds. He wished Carpenter would hurry up and pay him what he owed. Otherwise, he'd be forced to take out a loan. The thought weighed heavily on him, and by the time he wandered into the mudroom at sunset, he was grouchy, dirty and running on empty.

His belly rumbling, he wandered into the kitchen, where Mrs. Rutland was slipping into her jacket to go home. Sly pushed his worries away to focus on more pressing needs. "My mouth is watering. What did you make?"

"Beef stew," she said. "It's simmering, but should be ready in about half an hour. Be sure to soak the pan. I'll wash it in the morning. Your salad and a coconut cream pie are in the fridge, and that loaf of homemade bread on the counter is still warm."

Sly licked his lips. "What would I do without you?" he asked, and he was dead serious.

"Either learn to eat your own cooking, live on fast food or get married. I'll be here bright and early tomorrow."

"Thanks, Mrs. R."

After a quick shower, Sly stepped into clean clothes.

Barefoot, he took the stairs two at a time. In the kitchen he helped himself to a generous portion of stew and a thick slab of bread slathered with butter and jam.

As always, the food was delicious, but as much as Sly relished his solitude, tonight he wanted company to take his mind off his troubles. Female company, and not just any woman. Someone who would listen and understand, without making any demands on him. Lana.

He imagined packing up the meal and bringing it to her place to share with him. She'd insist that she was full, and then steal a piece of his buttered bread. She'd talk about her day and ask him about his.

Sly wasn't about to analyze his emotions. He knew what he wanted and that was that.

So what if they couldn't date or enjoy a short-term relationship? Who cared if their feelings for each other were too hot for friendship, or that they wanted different things? He could still drop by with dinner and say hello—if she was home.

He picked up his cell phone to find out.

"What if I'm pregnant?" Lana asked, propping her chin heavily on her fist. "What if I'm not?"

Several cartons of Chinese food from her favorite Chinese takeout sat between her and Kate on the breakfast-nook table. Normally she relished every bite and often had seconds. Tonight, she was too wound up to do more than pick at her meal.

"Which would you rather be—as if I didn't know?" Kate asked.

"Pregnant." Lana wanted that with her whole being. There was only one problem. "If I am, I'm going to have to tell Sly."

"Since he's the daddy-to-be, that's only fair."

"I suppose, but he won't be happy about it."

"He'll certainly be surprised, that's for sure. I'd want time to absorb a bombshell like this."

"Of course there's that. But once, when we were discussing having kids, Sly said he didn't want any. He raised his brother, and apparently that didn't turn out so well. He said that had been enough fathering for him."

"That was probably just talk." Looking thoughtful, Kate picked a crispy noodle from her plate and popped it into her mouth. "But suppose he doesn't want a child. What'll you do then?"

Lana had already decided that. "The same thing I've been planning to do for months now—raise him or her by myself. That is, *if* I'm pregnant. What if I'm not?"

"Here we go again," Kate muttered. "There's only one way to find out. Take. The. Test. You've been stalling since I walked in the door."

"Because we wanted to eat first." Because she was afraid.

Kate scoffed. "I'm the only one who ate. Let's do this."

"I guess it's time," Lana said. "After we clean up the dinner mess."

"It'll keep for a while. No more delay tactics. I want to find out if you're pregnant almost as badly as you do. So march your behind into the bathroom now, or I swear, I'll drag you in there."

Lana saluted. "Yes, ma'am."

Minutes later, Lana sat on the toilet lid, holding her breath while she waited for the results of the digital pregnancy test. Naturally, her cell phone rang. Several bars of Shenandoah's "Mama Knows" tinkled through the air.

Lana moaned. "That's my mother. She always did have impeccable timing. I'll let it go to voice mail."

In what seemed like seconds later, her cell phone rang again, this time without an identifying tune.

Kate, who was sitting cross-legged on the carpet just outside the open bathroom door, staring at the timer on her cell phone, glanced in the direction of Lana's phone. "You're popular tonight. You want me to pick that up for you?"

"Are you kidding? There's no way I can talk to anyone right now."

"At least let me check who it is." Kate grabbed the phone. Her eyes widened. "You won't believe this. It's Sly."

"I definitely can't talk to him," Lana wailed.

"Yeah, that would be really awkward." Kate set the phone down.

Feeling as if she would die if she didn't find out soon, Lana said, "How many seconds left?"

Kate checked the timer. "About seventy."

Those moments dragged on forever, but finally, the timer buzzed.

For all her impatience, Lana sat frozen in place.

"Well?" Kate asked. "Aren't you going to check the results?"

"I can't."

"Hand it over."

Kate studied the LED display with a blank expression. Uh-oh.

Lana's heart sank. She wasn't pregnant after all. "Bad news, huh?"

"Actually, it's the opposite." Kate beamed at her. "Congratulations, Lana. You're pregnant."

Certain she'd misheard, Lana shook her head. "Say that again?"

Kate held out the results for her to read. "In big, bold letters, it says *pregnant*. Congratulations, Lana. You're going to have a baby!"

Afraid to hope—she'd waited and suffered for so many years to be where she was now—Lana bit her lip. "Maybe I should take another test, just to make sure."

"The packaging and instructions claim that this test is ninety-nine-percent accurate, Lana."

"Which means there's a one-percent chance that it's wrong."

"All right, have it your way. But I'll bet my last paycheck that the next test results come out the same."

Lana had bought three different pregnancy test kits. She took all three, and every time the results were the same.

"I'm pregnant! I'm pregnant!" Laughing, she hugged Kate hard. "I never imagined this could happen to me."

"It seems all you needed was one night with a big, strong cowboy," Kate said. "And what a cowboy he is. Between your pretty face and his rugged features, you're going to have one gorgeous child."

The words sobered Lana. "Did you not hear what I said earlier? Sly doesn't want to be a father. And don't forget that only last Friday we decided not to see each other anymore. Then there's the lawsuit." She buried her face in her hands.

"Eventually the lawsuit will end," Kate said. "Maybe Sly changed his mind and wants to keep seeing you. He just called, right?"

"It was a mutual decision," Lana said.

"So what? This pregnancy changes everything."

"You're telling me. I can't even imagine what he'll do when he finds out. But it definitely won't be good."

"You can't be sure of that. When you discussed kids before, it was all hypothetical. This is real, Lana. A real baby the two of you created."

"But Sly and I don't love each other. We haven't known each other long enough to fall in love."

Kate waved her hand in the air in a dismissive gesture.

"You have the next seven or so months for that. Quit being so negative."

"I'm just scared."

"I know, sweetie. I would be, too. But no matter what happens, I'm here for you."

Profoundly grateful, Lana teared up. "You're such a great friend."

"Don't cry, or I will, too," Kate said, blinking furiously. "I'd like to open a bottle of wine and toast the pregnancy, but I guess that's out."

"For quite a while." Lana nibbled her thumbnail. "Sophie is supposed to come over on Saturday. What am I going to say to her? Sly is coming over, too, to help convince her that I'm right person to adopt her baby. I'm not sure I can handle telling either of them about this, let alone both. Then there's Sunday dinner with my parents and Liz and Eric...." Lana groaned.

"Slow down, Lana. You don't have to reveal anything just yet. In fact, you shouldn't. Just in case, you should see a doctor and talk to him or her."

Lana nodded. She would make an appointment with her gynecologist right away. "Promise me you won't say a word, Kate."

"I swear on my grandpa's grave." Kate crossed her heart. "I'll help you clean up the dinner stuff. Then, unless you want me to stick around, I'm heading home."

"I'll be fine. And I'll clean up. You've done enough."

At the door, Lana hugged her friend. "Thanks for being here for me."

"That's what best friends are for. I'll probably be awake for a few hours yet, so if you want to talk later, call me. And thanks for letting me be the first to share in your excitement."

As soon as the door shut behind Kate, Lana laughed out loud.

A baby!

FRIDAY AFTERNOON, SLY took a break from his usual chores and checked his watch. Lana hadn't returned his call from the other night, and he needed to know if she still wanted him to come over the next day. At least that was what he told himself. The truth was, he hadn't talked to her in a week. He missed her.

He waited until he figured she was home from work before reaching for his cell phone.

"Sorry I haven't called you back," she said. "I've been waiting to hear from Sophie."

"And?"

"Not a peep."

She sounded different somehow, but Sly couldn't put his finger on what had changed. Her voice, maybe. He guessed their decision not to see each other anymore had something to do with it. That and stressing about Sophie.

Wary now, he asked, "Have you changed your mind about me coming over tomorrow?"

"I hate for you to drive all the way over here if you don't have to."

Sly figured she was probably fidgeting the way she did when something bothered her. Everything hinged on whether Sophie showed up. He almost asked for the girl's phone number so that he could contact her and make sure she followed through. But he figured he should let Lana handle that. Otherwise, she'd probably bust his chops.

"Don't worry about Sophie," he said. "Trust me, she'll approve of your place and the neighborhood."

Lana's heavy sigh could mean anything.

"Are you still okay with the decision we made the other night?" he asked.

"You mean about not seeing each other anymore?" A long pause. "Are you?"

She hadn't answered the question, but if she wanted him to answer first, he would. "To be honest, no. I enjoy being with you." Dog that he was, he missed kissing her and fooling around.

"Okay, then," she answered, as if she hadn't heard what he'd said. "Why don't you come tomorrow around eleven-thirty."

Wishing he could read her mind, Sly agreed and disconnected.

Women. He just didn't get them.

Chapter Eleven

"Hey," Sly said when Lana answered the door late Saturday morning.

"Hi." Without meeting his eyes, she stepped aside and gestured him through the door.

He took in her stiff posture, solemn expression and too-pale skin and knew something was wrong.

"You okay?" he asked.

"Still shaking off a flu bug." She waved her hand toward the living room.

"When we talked yesterday, you didn't mention the flu."

"I came down with it last Sunday and it didn't seem important." Lana took the armchair, leaving him the sofa.

"I'm lucky I didn't catch it from you," he said.

Yeah, instead she'd given him a healthy dose of lust that was impossible to shake.

She gave a distracted nod. Her face, usually an open book, was drawn and tight, as her index finger traced and retraced a wavy line on the fabric of the armchair.

"Did you have to miss work?" Sly asked.

She gave him a puzzled look. "What?"

"Because of the flu."

"I took Wednesday off. Otherwise, I've been feeling okay."

She didn't seem okay now, not with the green tinge that

suddenly tinted her complexion. She appeared paler, too. More puzzling was the tension emanating from her.

Sly cleared his throat. "We've been real busy at the ranch. It seems that no matter how hard my crew and I work at it, there's always some length of fence to repair or replace. We've been digging ditches, too, because the old drainpipes aren't working anymore."

He wasn't about to mention Tim or the fact that, tired of waiting for her cousin to pay up, he'd stopped by the bank and picked up a dreaded loan application.

With an absent look, Lana attempted a smile that didn't quite make it. "I can't imagine."

Enough was enough. "Is it me being here, or is it waiting for Sophie that has you wound up so tight today?" Sly asked.

"Uh…" Her cell made the *blip* sound that meant she'd received a text message. She glanced at it and frowned. "What a surprise—Sophie won't be coming today after all."

She flicked a piece of lint from the knee of her jeans, her hair hanging like a curtain around her face, hiding her expression.

Sly could only imagine what she must be going through. "Let me guess—she wants to postpone for another week."

"Seems that way. And you drove all the way over here."

"No worries—I could use the break." Wanting to lighten the mood, he sniffed the air and licked his lips. "Whatever you're cooking smells great."

"It's a chicken recipe I got from my mother. Sophie ate a lot that day at Big Mama's, and I made a huge amount of food. What am I going to do with it all?"

"I'll help you out with that," Sly teased.

Instead of smiling, Lana nodded somberly. "It's just about ready."

The table was set for three. Sly helped bring the food to the table, and they sat down across from each other.

Lana had definitely put a big meal together—chicken wrapped in dough, curried fruit, salad and hot rolls. Sly dug in. "This is delicious," he said, licking his lips in appreciation.

Lana toyed with her plate of untouched food. "Thanks."

Sly set down his fork. "What's the deal, Lana? Since I've been here, you refuse to meet my eyes, you don't seem to hear what I say and you sure aren't talking much. Something's off."

With a sigh, she finally met his gaze. "You're right—I'm upset."

"About Sophie?"

"Her, too."

"So it's me you're upset with," he said, mentally smacking his forehead. *Of course.* "I tried to talk about us when I called last night, but you wouldn't. I meant what I said on the phone. I don't want you out of my life."

He hadn't planned to say that, hadn't even realized it was true until now. "If you're willing, we can work this out."

Finally she met his gaze, her expression bleak. Her hands twisted together in her lap. "Oh, Sly, I…"

She swallowed hard and with a sickening realization, it dawned on him—she'd met someone. He was a fool. "Who's the lucky guy?" he asked, keeping his tone and expression bland.

"Pardon me?"

"The man you're dating."

She looked puzzled. "I'm not dating anyone. If I were, I'd tell you."

Sly released the breath he'd been holding. "Then what's wrong?"

She jabbed her fork listlessly at her chicken before setting it down.

No appetite, pale… "You're still sick," he guessed.

Without answering , she nudged the chicken platter toward him. "Please, help yourself to seconds."

His belly was still empty, but he couldn't eat another bite. Not with the odd tension simmering in the air. "No, thanks," he said.

It was painfully obvious that she didn't want him around now that Sophie had canceled. That stung.

"Thanks for lunch." Sly pushed his chair away from the table and stood. "I should be on my way, and you should probably be in bed."

Lana searched his face, her eyes shadowed with indecision, and then sighed. "Don't go just yet, Sly. There's something I should tell you."

Ominous words. But she couldn't be dumping him— they weren't together. He sat down again. "Go ahead."

"I— Oh, jeez." She covered her mouth with her hand and bolted for the bathroom.

LANA FINALLY LET go of the toilet bowl and staggered to her feet. She washed her face and rinsed out her mouth. Although she was weak, she felt much better now. This part of pregnancy was no fun at all.

But telling Sly would be far worse.

He was sure to be shocked, unhappy and angry. Lana felt sick all over again.

Keeping the pregnancy to herself until after she met with her doctor seemed the smart thing to do, just in case the tests were wrong and she wasn't pregnant after all. Yet deep down, she was certain that she was.

As the baby's father, Sly deserved to know. Not after the doctor's appointment. Now.

Even if she was shaking clear to her toes.

Squaring her shoulders, she opened the bathroom door. Just outside, Sly was waiting for her. "How are you?"

"Better now."

He walked her to the living room and sat her down on the sofa with such care and gentleness that she wanted to weep. "Can I get you a glass of water?" he said.

"Yes, thanks."

While waiting for him to return from the kitchen, Lana steeled her courage.

He watched her closely as she drained the glass, reminding her of an anxious parent. After setting the glass aside, he sat down beside her, tucked her hair behind her ears and peered at her face. "You have more color now, but you should probably be in bed."

Oh, how she longed to do just that, burrow under the covers and forget all about sharing her news with Sly. But if she didn't say something to him now, she couldn't live with herself. "Forget about bed," she said. "I need to talk to you."

"So you said right before you threw up. Whatever it is can wait until you're better."

"No. You have to hear this now."

The somber expression on his face and the dark concern in his eyes tore at her. He may not want a relationship with her, but he cared.

"My God, you're really sick." Sly was rigid with dread.

Lana forgot her own fears. Wanting only to reassure him that she was healthy, she smoothed his furrowed forehead with a caress. "I promise you, I don't have cancer or any other disease."

"Thank God." He sagged against the sofa cushions, the relief on his face touching her deeply. "My mother died of cancer, and I don't wish that on anyone."

"You were eleven, right?" she asked.

He nodded. Lana couldn't imagine losing a parent, especially at such a tender age. Her worries at that age had centered on being popular and whether her mom would let her go to a sleepover.

Then to lose a father two years later… "That's so sad," she said.

"It was a long time ago." Sly pulled her hand to his lips and kissed her knuckles. "So it is just a bad flu."

She forced herself to meet his gaze. "It isn't the flu, either. I threw up because…" Knowing the world was about to change forever, she paused a moment. "Because I'm suffering from morning sickness."

"I… Huh?" The confusion on Sly's face was almost comical. But there was nothing funny about their situation.

"That's right, I'm pregnant." There. Her secret was out.

"Pregnant," Sly repeated with a stunned expression. "From that night?"

Lana nodded. "You're the only man I've been with."

"But you said you couldn't get pregnant."

"That's what I believed. My ex-husband and I tried for four years, first the normal way, then using artificial insemination. We didn't have any luck. Tests showed that I was the one who couldn't conceive. That's why Brent left me."

"The jerk." Sly scrubbed his hand over his face. "If you can't conceive, how can you possibly be pregnant?"

"Because miracles happen?"

"You're happy about this baby," he said, looking anything but.

Lana nodded. "I've wanted children for as long as I can remember, since I was a child myself."

Sly glanced at her stomach, which was still relatively flat. "When did you find out about this?"

"Wednesday—the night you called and I didn't answer. When the phone rang, I was waiting for the results of the first pregnancy test. I took two more to make sure. But even without the tests, I knew. I have all the symptoms."

Although her body still looked the same as always and she couldn't yet feel the life growing inside her, she already loved her baby.

Sly frowned. "You waited until now to tell me? What were you planning to do if Sophie had come over today? Spring it on us both together?" He barked out a laugh that totally lacked humor. "Oh, that would've been a real kick." He eyed her coolly. "It's obvious that you're keeping the baby."

She nodded.

"Do I get a say in this?"

His reaction was every bit as bad as Lana had expected. She hated the shuttered expression on his face and the cold look of betrayal in his eyes. Somehow she managed to keep her back straight and her chin high.

"If you don't want to be involved, I understand." She bit her lip. "I wasn't even going to say anything until I met with my doctor. In case…you know." She couldn't even say the words. "But I'm certain that I'm pregnant."

His expression unreadable, Sly gave a terse nod. "When is your appointment?"

"Tuesday after work." She planned to leave the day care early.

He blew out a heavy breath. "I can't believe this has happened. I always use condoms. Always. I wish to hell I'd used them that night."

Lana hadn't expected him to jump for joy, but his reaction hurt. She couldn't stop a bitter smile. "As I recall, you were in too much of a hurry to stop for protection."

"Because we're both clean and you assured me you couldn't get pregnant." Once again, he scrubbed his hands over his face. "If I'd suspected this could happen I would have taken the extra few minutes."

"And you think I wouldn't have? I didn't plan to get pregnant that night, Sly. But I won't lie—I'm aching for this baby, and I'm beyond grateful that I have a chance to be a mom. I'm also sorry that it happened this way, with neither of us having a say in what we wanted."

"That's something, at least." He rolled his shoulders as if they were too tight. "I need time to think."

Lana nodded.

With an odd, humorless smile, Sly stood. "I guess Sophie won't be coming over next weekend after all."

Lana hadn't thought that far ahead. "Probably not. Sly, I really am sorry for springing this on you."

"At least you told me."

She started to get up, but he gestured for her to stay put. "I can let myself out. I'll be in touch."

Hugging her waist, Lana stared at the empty fireplace until the door clicked shut behind him.

DETERMINED TO PUSH her troubles from her mind and keep the pregnancy from her family for a while, Lana pulled to a stop in front of her parents' house for Sunday dinner. Hoping to stave off any nausea, she'd gobbled a few crackers on the drive over. So far, so good.

It was a beautiful May day, the late-afternoon sun still high and warm, and she couldn't help but feel lighthearted. Not ready to endure lectures or scrutiny from her mother just yet, she headed around to the backyard.

As usual, her dad and Eric stood in front of the smoking grill. "Hey, guys," Lana said as she reached them. "Something sure smells wonderful."

Eric grinned. "Grandpa Jake's ribs always do."

The family recipe had been developed by their grandfather decades ago. "Fourth of July ribs in May?" Lana licked her lips. "What's the occasion?"

Instead of answering, Eric glanced at Lana's father to reply. Her father tapped his cheek for a kiss. "Hello, favorite oldest daughter." He winked. "You're looking especially pretty today."

Lana smiled. "Must be this new spring dress. Thanks, Dad."

Connor and Emma noticed her, shrieked and came running.

"What are you two up to today?" she asked after hugging them.

"We're playing hide-and-seek, but Emma always jumps up and shows me where she's hiding." Connor rolled his eyes. "Will you play with us, Lana?"

"Sure, but how about a little later? I want to visit with Grandpa and your dad. Then I'm pretty sure Grandma and your mom would appreciate my help with dinner."

"That reminds me," Lana's father said. "Your mother booked us a trip next weekend. We're driving over to Helena to visit Aunt Jessica. So no family dinner next week."

"Okay." Lana was secretly relieved. Keeping the pregnancy a secret wasn't going to be easy, and she could use the break.

She was chatting with Eric and her father when the kitchen door opened. To Lana's shock, Cousin Tim stepped outside.

Her jaw dropped. Of all the days for her surly cousin to visit… She was in no mood to face him. The mere sight of him made her remember the lawsuit and Sly, and right now, she didn't want to think about Sly or yesterday, or any of the secrets she was keeping from her family.

"What's he doing here?" she grumbled in a low voice.

Her father's eyebrows rose a fraction. "Come on, honey,

he's family. Didn't your mother tell you? She called yesterday and invited him to dinner."

That explained the ribs.

Her father gestured her cousin over. "Glad you could make it, Tim."

Lana's cousin joined them at the grill with his usual stiff nod. "That's some fancy grill. I see you're putting it to good use, making Grandpa Jake's ribs." He almost cracked a smile, making him appear much more approachable. "I haven't eaten ribs since last year's Fourth of July picnic. Before I forget, Michele says it's too nice to eat inside. She wants to eat out here."

"Great—we'll use the picnic table," Lana's father said. "It's been a few weeks since we touched base, Tim. How are things?"

"Lousy." Cousin Tim's jaw tightened. "That damn lawsuit…" He looked as if he could spit nails. "I figured out why Pettit's picking on me. He aims to bankrupt me, ruin my reputation and drive me off my land by making me pay for something I didn't do."

Cousin Tim had it all wrong. Sly would never do that. Lana warned herself to stay out of it, but the urge to defend Sly was too strong. "That's an awful thing to say," she retorted.

Her cousin seemed taken aback. She was just as surprised at herself, but unable to stop. "It's not as if he's asking for the sun and the moon. He wants restitution for the animals he lost and an apology."

"I sure as hell won't apologize for something I didn't do, and I won't pay, either."

Cousin Tim's thinned lips and fisted hands made Lana's knees shake, but this was important. "Have you ever actually made the effort to explain to Sly that you didn't do it?" she asked.

All three men stared at her, and she realized she'd referred to Sly by his first name. As if they had some sort of connection. Which they did, but her family had no idea about that.

She continued, "You and Sly—er, Mr. Pettit—have never really discussed the poisoning, have you? When he attempted to talk with you, you pointed a rifle at him and ordered him off your land. If you would just sit down and engage in a rational dialogue, you could work this out."

Cousin Tim's eyes narrowed. "Why are you defending him?"

Lana swallowed and came close to explaining exactly why. But this wasn't the right moment to reveal that she was carrying Sly Pettit's baby.

Imagining her family's shocked reaction to *that,* her stomach flip-flopped. So much for the crackers. *Oh, please, not a bout of morning sickness now.*

No, she decided. This sick feeling had nothing to do with morning sickness and everything to do with fear. She'd done what she dreaded most—stirred up family controversy. If she wanted to make it through the evening in one piece, she'd better keep her mouth shut.

Tim was waiting for her reply. "I've heard a few things," she hedged.

"What you've heard is wrong. Pettit outright accused me of poisoning his cattle, when I never did any such thing. I hope the bast—the so-and-so rots in hell."

Lana managed to bite her tongue, but she was sure her cold expression spoke volumes.

After a lengthy and somewhat tense silence, Eric cleared his throat. "Pretty amazing that the Grizzlies made it to the tournament this year. How do you figure they'll do next year, Tim?"

As the men launched into a lively conversation about

basketball, Lana released a silent sigh of relief. As much as she enjoyed the sport, she needed to escape. "I'm going to help Mom and Liz now," she said.

After promising the kids a game of hide-and-seek after the meal, Lana headed inside. Anything her mother said was preferable to listening to her cousin and fighting with herself to keep her mouth shut. Though why she was defending a man who now probably wanted nothing to do with her or their child, she had no idea.

Chapter Twelve

Sly's sister had invited him over for dinner Monday night. Not in the best mood, he debated canceling. A couple of times, he picked up the phone to do just that. But he was tired of being alone with his thoughts, thoughts that only seemed to go around in circles.

Lana was having a baby. *His* baby. He couldn't get his arms around that, was still numb with shock. But she seemed happy about it. Because she'd wanted a baby. Him, on the other hand… Sly didn't want a baby, didn't want to screw up his own kid like he had Seth.

Tough crap, huh? Whether he wanted to or not, he was having a kid.

He only hoped Lana hadn't told anyone. He didn't want the news spread around town just yet. And it would spread. Amy and Sheila and everyone else in Prosperity would make sure of that. Sly made a mental note to ask Lana not to say anything to anyone just yet.

Wanting to enjoy himself for a few hours, he arrived at Dani's place with a bottle of wine in hand.

"Hey, big brother." She hugged him. "I'm fresh out of wine and was hoping you'd bring a bottle."

Her cat, named Fluff for his white fur-ball appearance, meowed and butted Sly's calf for some attention. Sly bent down and scratched the cat just behind his head. "Hey there, big guy." Disapproving of the girlish name Dani had stuck the male cat with, he never used it.

The animal purred happily.

Sly sniffed the air. "Do I smell homemade mac and cheese?"

Dani nodded. "With ground beef."

As much as he loved the stuff, he knew what it meant. "Uh-oh—your trademark breakup dish. This can't be about Cal—you two split up weeks ago. Who's the bum this time?"

Dani filled two glasses with wine and handed him one. "I wasn't planning to go into that just yet. I'd rather talk about something else."

"May as well get it out of the way." He straddled a chair backward at her little kitchen table. The twenty-pound cat jumped onto his lap.

"All right, we'll get it out of the way." Dani plunked into the other chair and raised her glass. "But first, a toast. Here's to a fun evening together—eventually."

She had no idea how bad Sly needed fun. He saluted with his glass. "I'll drink to that."

When they set down their drinks, Dani sighed and got right to it. "Paul dumped me."

"I know he took you home that night we played pool at Clancy's, but I didn't realize you two were seeing each other."

"We were."

"I'm glad to hear he's out of your life. He was bad news."

"I didn't think so." Dani picked at the label on the bottle. "I really liked him."

"I have no idea why. He wasn't good enough for you."

"You say that about every guy I date."

"Because it's true."

"Hey, I don't do that to you." When Sly didn't comment, she added, "At least I'm out there, trying. You aren't even dating."

His errant thoughts wandered to Lana. The baby. He wished to hell that—

"What's wrong?" Dani asked.

"Nothing." He schooled his expression into bland calmness, but his sister appeared unconvinced. He couldn't fool her.

"Nothing I'm ready to talk about. Let me top off that wine."

Dani held out her glass. "So I have to talk about my problems but you don't have to share yours? No fair."

"Too bad."

"Stubborn man. Fine. How's the lawsuit going?"

"At the moment, nothing is happening."

"Bummer," she said with sympathy. "Now what?"

Sly thought about the loan application he had yet to fill out. Dammit, he couldn't really afford the added debt, especially with Lana pregnant. Because the one thing he knew was that he wasn't going to let her pick up the tab for anything.

Carpenter *had* to pay up, period.

Sly wanted his money *now*. He didn't hide his impatience. "I wait while my attorney and his go round and round."

"It's taking forever, and you need that new drainage system."

"Yep."

"At least the weather is dry now. It could stay this way for months. Maybe you can put off spending the money for a while."

"Yep."

She gave him a worried look. "Can't you try talking to Tim Carpenter again?"

"And get shot? He's just mean enough to make good on that threat. No, thanks."

"This is how long-term feuds start. I'm thinking the Hatfields and the McCoys."

Sly shrugged. "It is what it is."

His sister examined him closely, then fixed him with her pit-bull stare. "Something else is bothering you, brother mine. Spill."

Just a little thing. Lana was pregnant with his baby. Sly slid his wineglass around. "I'm dying of starvation here. Is that mac and cheese about ready?"

"You won't talk. Message received, but only because I'm starving, too."

The next few minutes were filled with setting the table, serving up and eating.

Wanting food, Fluff jumped onto Sly's lap again and butted his hand, begging shamelessly. Sly gave the cat a hunk of ground beef, then pushed the beggar off his lap.

"Have you talked to Lana lately?" Dani asked a while later when they'd both taken the edge off.

Here we go. Sly swallowed a mouthful of food and chased it with wine before replying, "Saw her Saturday."

His sister's expression brightened. "You went out?"

He shook his head.

"Dang, I wish that lawsuit was over so you could date. But you saw her?"

"I went over to her place because Sophie was supposed to come over. Then at the last minute, she baled. Again."

His sister made a sympathetic sound. "Lana must have been so upset. She's dying for a baby of her own. I wonder why Sophie keeps flaking out."

One thing was certain—Lana hadn't told Dani about the pregnancy yet. That was a relief. Sly wanted to be the one to give his sister the news. But first he needed more time to come to grips with the whole thing and figure out what to do about it. Right now, he didn't want to talk about Sophie or babies.

"How's work?" he asked.

"Tourist season is revving up and we're busier than ever. Which reminds me—guess who showed up for Sunday brunch with a big announcement?"

Sly didn't even try to guess and didn't have to wait long for the answer. Lit up with excitement, Dani blurted the news. "Rayna and Troy Madison. After five years of marriage, they're finally expecting!"

Sly knew the couple. They owned a local real estate company. Dani launched into the particulars and said something about a baby shower.

Pregnancy and babies. They seemed to be everywhere. "Must be in the air," Sly muttered.

"Pardon me?"

"I said, if they're happy, that's good news."

"Of course they're happy. Like Lana, Rayna's been wanting a baby for a while now. I sure hope that Lana will—"

"Could we not talk about Lana anymore?"

Dani's eyes narrowed a fraction and she gave him a canny look. "You can tell me about it, Sly. I'm a great listener, and I won't say anything to anyone."

She *was* a great listener, but Sly wasn't about to say squat about his situation. The pregnancy was new and tenuous, and he was still feeling sucker punched. Besides, as true-blue as Dani was, she never had been able to keep secrets for long. God knew who she'd spill the news to. Plus, she and Lana were friends. Whatever he said to Dani might get back to Lana.

Sly wasn't taking any chances. "I sure am hungry tonight." He refilled his plate and began to eat.

Dani looked genuinely concerned. "I don't understand why you won't talk about Lana."

Sly frowned. "Why are you so vested in the idea of Lana and me together?"

"Because she's great and you're great. You two *should* be together."

Sometimes his sister drove him crazy. "I don't need a matchmaker," he growled before returning to his meal.

"Jeez, you're touchy. All right, let's talk about the weather. It's been pretty nice lately. After the winter we had, you and all the other ranchers in Prosperity must be pretty happy. Especially with the decent rainfall and sunshine this spring. And let's see, there was an article in yesterday's paper about local tourism. This year it should be up again, for the third year in a row.

"Oh, and starting a week from Friday the mall will host a huge Memorial Day weekend sale. I'm planning to call she-who-you-do-not-want-me-to-mention and invite her and her best friend, Kate, to go shopping with me. Fascinating stuff, huh?"

"As long as you three don't talk about me." Sly kept his eyes on his rapidly emptying plate.

"I can't promise you that. Wow, you polished off your second helping fast. Going for thirds?"

He shook his head and decided to call it an early night. "Come on, I'll give you a hand cleaning up."

While he helped Dani with the dishes, his thoughts circled to Lana again. She'd mentioned a doctor's appointment tomorrow. Sly wanted to know what the doctor said, and how Lana was feeling. That morning sickness stuff seemed brutal. He decided to call her tomorrow evening and find out.

"—for ice cream," Dani was saying. "I'm in the mood

for some rocky road. Let's go to Lannigan's Ice Creamery and get ourselves a couple of cones."

The ice creamery was one of Sly's favorites. As tempted as he was, he was ready for solitude. He shook his head. "I'm beat, and tomorrow's another busy day."

"I have to get to bed early, too, but it's such a warm, beautiful evening, and I have my heart set on rocky-road ice cream. I need the sugar hit, and by your long face, so do you."

"Another time." Sly handed her a bill. "Get yourself a treat on me."

Dani refused the money. "All right, I'll go by myself and enjoy my ice cream without you. But I sure hope you cheer up soon. You're a lot more fun when you're in a good mood. My gut feeling is that this has something to do with Lana."

"Yeah? Well, my gut is telling me it's full." He patted his belly.

"Ha-ha. I'm serious about this. If you'd just quit fighting yourself and accept that Lana is the right woman for you, your life would be so much better."

"Thank you, Dr. Dani."

Dani bowed from the waist. "Anytime. I hope you're listening to me. Work things out with her."

He wasn't sure that was possible. Lana was pregnant, and the baby was his.

What the hell was he supposed to do now?

A few hours after her ob-gyn appointment, Lana relaxed at home with a book on pregnancy. Her intention was to devour every word, but she was so elated, so excited, that she could barely concentrate.

What a shame she couldn't share the joy with Sly. She hadn't heard a word from him since she'd revealed that she was pregnant, and figured he was still coming to grips with the idea.

Over the past few days she'd realized that no matter where life took either of them, she wanted him to be part of their child's life. Of course, that choice was his, and she wasn't going to pressure him.

Suddenly her cell phone rang. The screen said Sly Pettit. Lana's heart bumped happily, yet in the same instant, she was worried what he might say. She answered cautiously. "Hi, Sly."

"Hey," he said in the deep voice that usually made her hum inside.

Not tonight. She was too nervous. She caught her breath and waited.

"You saw the doctor today," he said.

"Dr. Valentine. That's right."

"And?"

"She called the pregnancy a miracle. Everything appears normal." The smile Lana had worn since that moment deepened.

Sly's relieved exhale told her that he'd been wondering and maybe worrying. A hopeful sign that maybe he had some feelings for their baby.

"How's the morning sickness?" he asked.

"The same. I've been eating crackers between meals, but Dr. Valentine suggested I also keep a supply by the bed to eat before I get up in the morning. I'll try that tomorrow. She also said that by the second trimester of pregnancy, when I'm about four months along, the morning sickness should disappear. So in another five or six weeks, I'll be fine."

"That's a long time to feel nauseated."

A small price to pay for the gift of life inside her. "I'll

survive. By the way, the baby's due date is January second next year."

Sly's reply was more a gruff sound than a word. Lana's heart sank. He wasn't on board about this baby after all. Not yet anyway.

She bit her lip. "I know you're not pleased about this, Sly, but I'm thrilled. And I want to reassure you that I don't expect anything from you. But if you want to be part of the baby's life…" She let the words trail off.

"I'm not sure what I want yet, except that I'm not going to abandon my own kid."

He sounded surly and overburdened. Lana closed her eyes against a wave of sadness. "Have you thought about how you want to be involved?"

"Like I said, I haven't figured that out yet."

"There's no rush. The baby isn't due for another seven and a half months, which gives you plenty of time to figure out what you want to do."

"Those months will go by fast. We need to talk more about this, a lot more."

Lana agreed. "Just tell me when and where."

"It's real busy around here right now, so it'll be a while."

"Got it." In the meantime, she would continue to fix up the nursery, read the baby books and shop for baby supplies.

"Have you told anyone?" Sly asked.

"Just my best friend, Kate. You met her at the Bitter & Sweet. She was here when I took the pregnancy test. She promised not to say anything, and I'm positive I can trust her."

"No one in your family knows?"

"Not yet," Lana said. "I'm not ready. When the time comes, I'll do it the same way I did with my decision to adopt. First I'll tell my sister and her husband, and then my parents."

She dreaded that, even more than when she'd explained her decision to adopt. "They'll be surprised. Happy that I'm able to conceive when we all were convinced that I couldn't. But they won't be pleased about the way it happened— they're kind of old-fashioned and think marriage should come before the baby."

"So I should expect your dad to come after me with a shotgun?"

"They aren't that bad. They just… It's going to take a while for them to get used to the idea."

"Tell me about it," Sly muttered. "Do *you* think two people should get married before they have a baby?"

"In a perfect world, yes."

"What about us?"

Lana wasn't about to lie. "I'm not ready for marriage."

Sly exhaled loudly, his relief clear. "Me, either. Wait till your folks find out I'm the baby's father."

"There's that, too." Imagining their reaction, Lana shuddered. A root canal would be more pleasant.

"Dani doesn't know yet, either," Sly said.

"I'm going with her and Kate to the mall in a week or so. Should I give her the news?"

"She mentioned your get-together. But no, I'll tell her. For now, let's keep it to ourselves."

Keeping the news from Dani wouldn't be easy, but if Sly wanted it that way… "Okay," Lana said. "Let's agree to keep this to ourselves for a few more weeks."

"Works for me. Just give me a heads-up when you're ready to spread the news around. I don't want my sister finding out from someone else. What about Sophie? Have you talked to her?"

"Not yet. I guess I should call her tonight."

"What are you going to say?"

Lana wasn't sure. "I'll come up with something. By the

way, Sunday night I went to my parents' for dinner, expecting to see just my sister and her family. But my mother invited someone else without warning me. Care to guess who came to dinner?"

"Just say it."

"Your favorite person—Cousin Tim."

Sly swore. "Must have been one hell of a rotten evening."

Lana recalled her cousin's negative attitude and the bad things he'd said about Sly. During dinner, she'd sat as far from him as possible and had attempted to ignore him. Still, she hadn't been able to enjoy Connor or Emma, and Grandpa Jake's ribs could have been dog meat for all she'd have noticed. "It wasn't fun," she said.

"I'll bet he called me a bunch of names."

"Among other things. He claims he didn't poison your livestock, Sly."

"Which is more than he ever told me."

"That's why I suggested he sit down with you and talk about it instead of running you off his land with his shotgun."

"You said that to him?" Sly sounded incredulous.

She'd also wanted to bolt and run, but she wasn't going to admit that. "Someone had to."

"I'll bet he loved that. Now you have a taste of what I've put up with all these months."

"I wish you two would work it out," Lana said.

"You sound just like Dani."

"I'll take that as a compliment. When she finds out about the baby, do you think she'll be happy?"

"Probably. We had dinner last night and she kept mentioning you. She believes we belong together." Sly sounded as if he was rolling his eyes.

Lana wished that was true, but they wanted different

things. "She mentioned you'd had dinner together when she called last night."

"What else did she say?" Sly asked.

"Nothing much, except that you weren't your usual self."

"Yeah, well, I'm still in shock. It didn't help that she kept nagging me about you."

Despite Sly's grudging words, Lana detected a teasing smile in his voice. "What did you tell her?" she asked.

"To butt out."

Picturing that, she grinned. "Hey, are you interested in coming to my next doctor's appointment?"

"Why would you need another appointment? Unless something's wrong. You said everything was fine."

For all his talk about not wanting a child, he sounded just like a worried father. Lana took heart from that. "As a pregnant woman, I'll be seeing Dr. Valentine every month for a checkup," she explained. "Then during the last month of pregnancy, I'll go every week. That's how she gauges how I'm doing, and how close to the due date I really am."

"I didn't know that," Sly said. "I only know about pregnant cows."

Lana laughed. A blink later, for the first time in what seemed forever, Sly actually chuckled.

"When is the next appointment?" he asked.

"A month from now, on a Tuesday. If you want to come, you're welcome."

"I'll get back to you on that."

Lana took heart from his words. At least he hadn't said no.

Chapter Thirteen

As soon as Lana disconnected from Sly, she called Sophie.

The girl sounded surprised to hear from her. "I was just about to text you."

"Let me guess—you're going to cancel our get-together next Saturday."

"Um…yeah," Sophie admitted in a sheepish voice. "How did you know?"

"You've done it twice already, and I figured…" Lana wasn't about to get into a blame game. "Why don't you tell me what you were going to text."

"Can I just send the text instead? It's kind of hard to say."

"Say it anyway."

"Okay. I, um, sort of decided that the Andersons should adopt my baby."

Lana had already guessed as much.

"It's just, they're a couple," Sophie went on. "And as my social worker says it's easier for a couple to raise a child than a single parent."

"That's true, but even without a partner, I believe in my heart and soul that I'll be a terrific mother," Lana said.

"You will. But I've been thinking about this a lot. My mom did okay with me, but I kinda missed not having a dad, you know?"

Lana couldn't even imagine. "If I was in your shoes, I'm sure I would," she admitted.

After losing his own father, Sly surely realized the same thing. Lana hoped he remembered that when he decided how he wanted to be involved in their son's or daughter's life. They didn't have to live together or even have a romantic relationship—although she wanted that, if the lawsuit ever settled—in order to both participate in raising their child.

"Are you mad?" Sophie asked.

If not for her own pregnancy, Lana would have been crushed. "I think the Andersons are very lucky people to become the parents of your baby."

"You do?"

"Absolutely."

"I didn't expect you to be okay about this. You're really nice, Lana. I hope that someday you'll get a baby."

"Thanks. That means a lot." Lana was dying to tell the girl that she was pregnant, but because of the agreement with Sly, she didn't. "Take good care of yourself, Sophie. I wish you a very bright future."

"You, too."

AFTER A GRUELING day spent moving six hundred head of cattle to the pastures with the greenest grasses, Sly was beat. So was Bee.

"You worked hard today, girl," he said as he brushed the horse down. Soothing work he enjoyed almost as much as Bee.

Slanting sunlight filtered through the barn windows, and the scents of leather, hay and animal filled the lofty space—some of Sly's favorite smells.

"I'll bet you're glad today is Friday," he added. "I sure am."

The horse nickered and seemed to nod. When Sly finished brushing her, he led her to her stall. On the way, she butted his backside playfully.

"Want a treat, do you?" Chuckling, he dug a carrot from his shirt pocket and offered it to her.

Bee took it straight from his palm. They had an understanding of sorts. She let him ride her hard whenever the need arose, saddled up or bareback. In return, she asked only for food, exercise, a good brushing and a daily carrot or two.

Why couldn't all women be as easy as Bee?

Sly snickered at that. Plenty of women were easy enough.

But not the one who mattered.

He hadn't spoken to Lana in over a week, not since her doctor's appointment. She was giving him the space he'd asked for, and he was grateful. At the same time, he felt like a jerk for keeping his distance.

It was his turn at bat. Trouble was, he still wasn't sure whether to bunt or hit a home run.

He was latching Bee's stall shut when Ollie entered the barn. Stetson in hand, he trudged toward Sly without his usual cocky swagger. He'd been unusually quiet all day.

Sly frowned. "It's Friday afternoon and you're free until Monday. I was sure that by now you'd be showered, changed and on your way to pick up your girlfriend."

"We didn't make any plans."

"You sick?"

"Uh-uh." Ollie shifted his weight. "I gotta talk to you."

Curious as to what was eating the guy, Sly gestured him to a worn bench along the planking. Nearby, reins and bits and other horse tacking hung on hooks. "What's on your mind?" he asked when they were both seated.

Ollie kicked the wall with the heels of his boots. "I got a problem."

"Something you want extra time off for," Sly asked. As

busy as the ranch was just now, he wasn't sure he could afford to give that to anyone.

"Not exactly." Ollie pulled a toothpick from his shirt pocket and stuck it between his teeth. For some reason, the toothpick made him appear more like a boy trying to be a man than an actual man.

Tired, hungry and wanting a shower, Sly prodded him along. "Spit it out, Ollie."

The kid tugged at the collar of his T-shirt, as if it was too tight. "Tiff—my girlfriend? Well, we just found out that she's pregnant."

He didn't look at all happy about that. Sly understood just how he felt. "I take it this isn't good news," he said.

"It sucks. Tiff wants to keep the baby and raise it. I don't."

This sounded, oh, so familiar. Sly eyed him. "What are you going to do?"

"That's what I'm here to talk to you about. I'm giving you my notice."

"Hold on, there. You signed on through September," Sly reminded him. He liked the kid and had been considering offering him a permanent job.

"I said I'd stay, but now I have to leave town."

"What does Tiff think of that?"

"Haven't told her." Ollie tossed the toothpick into the nearby trash barrel.

"Let me get this straight. Your girlfriend is pregnant with your baby, and you're going to walk out on her? I'm guessing without even a goodbye."

"That's the plan." Ollie's voice cracked.

"It's a bad plan, one you need to rethink. Instead of running away, be a man and deal with the situation."

Stern words, but Ollie needed to hear them. With a shock, Sly realized he was also talking to himself.

God knew he had his faults, but he'd always prided himself on taking responsibility for his actions. Lately, though, he'd done the opposite, just the way Seth used to.

Damn.

Sly was not his brother. He didn't run away from trouble.

Or did he? Sure as hell, he'd been trying to run from the idea of being a father. The realization made him frown.

"Don't look at me like that," Ollie said. "I'm only twenty—way too young to start a family."

"You should have thought about that when you and Tiff had unprotected sex."

"You get how it is, man. There comes a point when you're too far gone to keep your head on straight. Besides, she said it was her safe time."

"I hear you," Sly said. "No matter what a woman tells you, always use protection. I do."

Except for that one night with Lana.

"Look, this is a busy season at the ranch," he went on. "I need your help. Why don't you stick around for another week and think it over?"

"But I ain't ready to be a daddy."

"You're going to be one anyway." He let that hang in the air a few moments. "At least talk to Tiff. You owe her that much. Maybe you two can work something out."

"I guess I could do that," Ollie said with a grudging shrug. "But I'm only sticking around for another week." He left the barn.

Sly stayed. Too restless to sit, he paced around without really seeing the horse stalls or bales of hay stacked against the wall. It'd been almost a week since Lana had told him she was pregnant. Instead of thinking about her and the baby, he'd spent all of those days focused on himself and how he'd screwed up with Seth.

For years he'd assured himself that he would never saddle a kid with his poor example of a father. But life had turned on him, and Lana was pregnant with his baby and she was determined to raise it. Which made Sly no different from Ollie. Like the kid, he needed to man up and face his responsibilities.

Looking at situation that way, Sly realized what he had to do. Right there in the barn, he pulled his cell phone from his pocket and called Lana.

The phone rang four times, then went to voice mail. He left a message. "The Memorial Day weekend is right around the corner. If you're free a week from Saturday, I'd like to take you to dinner." Knowing what'd she say to that he added, "This won't be a date. We have to talk about our situation and we both need to eat. Why not over dinner? Call me back."

Sly disconnected. Feeling lighter than he had in days, he whistled as he exited the barn.

DANI WANTED NEW shoes, and after a quick dinner the Friday of the Memorial Day weekend holiday, Lana and Kate headed to the mall to meet her. Thanks to the mall-wide sale, the parking lot was full.

"Don't mention the pregnancy," Lana warned Kate as she searched for a place to park.

Her friend gave her a puzzled look. "You're keeping it a secret from Sly's sister?"

"Sly wants to tell her himself, but he isn't ready yet. I'm not ready to say anything to my family, either. We agreed to wait a while. Oh, and you also can't mention the dinner tomorrow night."

Kate made a face. "You're not leaving much to talk about."

"Sure I am. Guys you're dating, guys she's dating, shopping, food. What else is there?" Lana teased.

"That'll work. What do you think Sly will say when you go out tomorrow night?"

"I have no idea, and it isn't a date," Lana reminded her.

For now it was enough that he wanted to get together and talk. At last she spied a parking space. "We're meeting Dani at Altman's," she said as she maneuvered the car into the space.

Kate rubbed her hands together in anticipation. "I love that department store, and they have great shoes."

Ten minutes later, the three of them entered the women's shoe section. Dani went straight for the sandals.

"What do you think of these?" she asked, showing Lana and Kate a yellow strappy sandal with three-inch heels. "I have the cutest sundress to wear them with."

Lana loved them. "They're really sexy, but too high for me. If I tried to walk in those, I'd probably fall flat on my behind."

"No, you wouldn't," Kate said. "I want a pair, too, in red. So, Dani, is there a special guy you want to wear them for?"

Dani sighed. "I just went through a breakup."

Lana felt for her, but she was also confused. "When we met for coffee, you weren't seriously involved with anyone."

"As with most of my relationships, it didn't last long. But hey, if I wear these, some cute guy is bound to ask me out. Why don't we each try on a different color?"

Kate nodded. "I'm in. This way, Lana, you can test them out and see if you can walk in them."

A few minutes later, Lana admired herself in the mirror. "Yay, me," she said, very pleased with herself and the silver sandals. "I've walked to the wall and back and haven't stumbled or fallen over. And wow, look at my legs."

"Very sexy." Kate grinned. "If I were you, I'd wear them tomorrow night."

Dani's eyes widened. "You have a date tomorrow night! Who with?"

Lana glared at Kate. Her friend shrugged. "Hey, I didn't say anything."

"It's not an actual date," Lana explained. "Sly and I—"

"You and my brother are finally going out? Score!"

"I repeat, it isn't a date," Lana stated firmly. "We're getting together to talk—that's all."

"Sounds like a date to me." Dani looked like the cat who'd swallowed the canary. "You should definitely wear those sandals."

Lana itched to tell her about the pregnancy, but she'd given Sly her word. Things between them were precarious enough without her breaking her promise. She rolled her eyes. "Fine, I'll buy them. But it isn't a date."

Chapter Fourteen

Wishing she could relax with a glass of wine instead of making due with sparkling water, Lana sat across the table from Sly at an Italian restaurant on the outskirts of town. The out-of-the-way eatery was packed, and diners filled every table. Carpeting and acoustic ceiling tiles muted the noise level, and dim lighting, linen tablecloths and generous spacing between the tables added an air of privacy. Sly had chosen the perfect place for them to talk over dinner.

Lana was glad she'd dressed up in a silk sheath and, yes, the new silver sandals. Sly had also dressed up. In dark pants, a pressed shirt and tie, he was movie-star handsome. But then, he also looked great in jeans and a T-shirt.

"I've never eaten here before," she said. "How did you find this place?"

"A couple years ago, I stopped here for lunch on the way home from a cattle auction. The owner's mother makes the pasta from scratch using old family recipes. I think you'll like it."

Lana was already salivating. "I'm sure I will."

"I also figured that way out here in the boonies, there's less of a chance we'll run into family."

He'd thought of everything. On the forty-minute drive here, they'd made small talk. Lana had shared that Dani had assumed they were on a date tonight, which had caused some muttering. Then she'd updated Sly on her phone call with Sophie and shared a funny story about one of the kids at the day care, a boy who'd pretended he was a dog all week, barking and crawling around.

"Does he have mental problems?" Sly asked.

Lana shook her head. "He's fine, just quirky. Some kids are."

"I once had a dog who believed he was a person," Sly commented, his lips curling into a smile. "He was quirky, too."

He told Lana about a run-in with a coyote and the family of meadowlarks that had hatched in his backyard.

It was a conversation any couple on a date might have. Except this wasn't a date. They were here to talk about the baby—or so Lana thought. Waiting for the *real* conversation was nerve-racking. But she wanted to give Sly the space he deserved.

Meanwhile, doubts ate at her. What if he wanted nothing to do with her or their child? She felt an anxiety that all but killed her appetite. But if that was the case, she doubted they'd be sitting in this nice restaurant, having a nondate.

The waiter delivered the salads.

"Remember, we're going Dutch treat," she reminded Sly as they reached for their forks.

He nodded.

"I haven't heard lately—what's happening with the lawsuit?" she asked, wanting to know.

"Not a damn thing." He snorted in frustration.

"What's taking so long?"

"Your cousin. He's stalling. My attorney is doing what he can, but I'm about out of patience."

"Cousin Tim is about as easy to budge as a boulder," Lana said.

"On that, we both agree."

A short while later, the waiter removed their salad plates

and placed their dinner in front of them. "I don't want to talk about the lawsuit anymore," Sly said. "I want to enjoy this meal."

Throughout the delicious main course, Sly steered the conversation away from serious matters and kept things light and easy. Despite the amazing food, Lana's frustration level grew until she wanted to scream. Why wouldn't he get to the point?

Finally, the waiter cleared their plates. "Dessert?" he asked.

Lana shook her head, but Sly ordered coffee, tiramisu and two forks.

When the dessert arrived, Sly nudged the plate between them. "Half of this is yours."

"I'm too nervous, Sly." *And too impatient to wait one more second.* "I feel like there's an elephant in the room. You invited me to dinner to talk and I've been giving you space to bring up our situation when you're ready, and I'm frustrated."

With a somber expression, he set down his fork. "I was planning to wait until after the meal, but if you'd rather talk now, it's okay by me. I made a decision about the baby." He paused, his steady gaze revealing little.

If only Lana could read his mind. He claimed that he didn't want to abandon their child, but for all she knew, his idea of sticking around could be to offer monetary support and nothing more.

Aware of how he felt about having a child, she assumed that had to be it. Disappointed, but determined not to let on, Lana widened her eyes. "What did you decide?"

"I want to be part of his life."

She was surprised, and so relieved she sagged in her seat.

His expression confused, Sly scrutinized her. "You're not happy about that."

"Just the opposite. I'm so glad our baby will have the chance to get to know his or her daddy. What do you have in mind?"

"I'm still working on that, but for starters, I'll go with you to your next doctor's appointment. If the offer is still open."

"It is. It's going to be a very special appointment. We'll get to hear the baby's heartbeat."

Sly didn't exactly seem excited, but at least he'd agreed to be there. It was a beginning, and Lana decided she'd do whatever she could to encourage him.

"What time should I pick you up?" he said.

"Since I'll be coming straight from work, it'll be easier if we meet at the clinic."

He nodded. "Give me the details and I'll be there."

Lana gave him the information, then picked up her fork. "Now I'm ready to eat some of that tiramisu."

"WE WERE SUPPOSED to split the bill," Lana said as Sly pulled onto the highway and headed toward her place. "You should have let me pay my share."

Despite her words, she didn't seem too upset that he'd insisted on paying. The truth was, she hadn't stopped smiling since he'd announced he wanted to be part of the baby's life.

His chest was full and warm. Maybe he didn't want a kid, but he felt good that his decision had made her happy. He wasn't about to analyze why that was so important. It just was.

Darkness had fallen, but in the faint light of the dash he caught that soft smile. Desire slammed into him. If not for the truck's bucket seats, he'd have pulled Lana close and snuggled her against his side.

But that wasn't what tonight was about, and if he was smart, he'd spend the rest of the evening pissed off at her cousin or thinking about how being a father would mess with his life. Or anything to keep his mind off sex.

Unfortunately, his body wasn't cooperating. It wanted other things—specifically, to get nice and close to Lana. Fighting the hunger wasn't easy, but Sly was damned if he'd give in.

"You pay next time," he said.

"I'm going to hold you to that."

They were both quiet, until out of the blue she turned to him. "You'll make a great father, Sly. I know it."

He wasn't at all sure of that, but since he was going to be a father regardless, he intended to do much better with this kid than he had with Seth.

"When are you breaking the news to your family?" he asked.

The smile he so liked disappeared. "Probably after the next doctor's appointment."

It was as clear as day that she wasn't looking forward to that.

For the rest of the drive, they rode along in comfortable silence while the radio spit out a steady stream of rock 'n' roll and country-and-western songs.

When Sly stole a glance at Lana sometime later, he saw that she'd fallen asleep. He lowered the radio volume. At last, he pulled up in front of her town house and shut off the truck.

Reluctantly he woke her. "Lana, honey, we're here."

"Hmm?" She yawned and stretched, then smiled at him, her eyes unfocused and drowsy. "I guess I fell asleep. It's the pregnancy—I'm always tired." She frowned at the front of her dress. "I must have spilled something on myself."

The tender feelings that stirred in Sly's chest were new to him and difficult to understand. He gave her a goofy smile and blurted the first thing that came to mind. "That's just a little slobber. You slept with your mouth hanging open."

"I didn't. I'm so embarrassed."

"You looked cute."

For a moment he lost himself in her warm eyes, forgetting where he was and what he was doing. All that mattered was being here with Lana.

That worried him on several levels. He didn't like his strong feelings and didn't want her to get the wrong idea and assume he was getting serious about her. He wasn't.

Sly was wondering how fast he could make an exit without being a jerk when the raw desire on her face stopped him.

Fresh hunger roared through him. No, not fresh. His desire for Lana was a constant simmer inside him. It had just flared up. He'd never wanted a woman so much.

He glanced away, grateful for the lights around the townhouse complex and for the people still outside after ten at night. They had no idea how bad he needed chaperoning.

"Thanks for everything, Sly," she said. "For your decision to be a part of our baby's life and for a really great dinner."

"Sure," he said, once again all warm in his chest. "I'll walk you to your door."

"Don't bother. It's only twenty feet away, and you see all the neighbors out and about. Besides, this isn't a date, remember?"

The manners his parents had once taught him wouldn't allow that. "I don't care what it is," he said. "I'm walking you to your door."

"Stubborn cowboy." She let out a soft laugh. "All right, walk me if you must."

By the time he rounded the truck and reached the passenger side, Lana was standing beside it, waiting for him.

Her dress clung to her curves and showed a good length of leg. Her skimpy little sandals made her legs seem impossibly long.

Sly itched to run his hands up her calves and thighs. All the way up...

Hardly aware of what he was doing, he slipped his arm around her and shortened his stride so that his steps matched hers.

It was a warm night and her silk dress had tiny sleeves that barely covered her shoulders. Her skin was smooth under his hand, and the faint scent of lavender he'd come to associate with Lana filled his senses.

His whole body tightened. If not for the unsuspecting chaperones all around, he would have stopped right here, pulled her to him and kissed her until they were both out of their minds.

Stepping onto her little concrete slab of a porch, she faced him. "This was the best nondate I've ever had."

"You go on a lot of those, do you?" he said, his lips twitching.

Laughing, she placed her hand on her barely rounded stomach for a nanosecond. It was long enough to draw Sly's attention.

He sobered. "You touched your belly a lot tonight. Does it hurt?"

"Not at all. I'm hardly aware that I'm doing it. I just— It's because I'm growing a baby, and I still can't quite believe it."

The joy on her face was something to see. "May I touch?" he asked.

Her smile broadened. "Sure, but you won't feel anything yet. It's too early. We should probably go inside first. Lord knows what the neighbors might think if they notice your hand on my stomach."

Sly told himself to remain outside, where they were both safe. But when she unlocked the door, he followed her inside.

She stopped in the entry and turned to him. "Now you can touch me."

He gently placed his palm against her stomach. Her silk dress was thin, and through it he touched her navel and her warmth. Maybe he didn't feel the baby, but he felt plenty. He was lit up from the inside out. Not the same kind of heat as sexual desire. This was different.

"You're right—I don't notice anything different," he said, his voice husky from his tender emotions. "You sure don't have much of a belly yet."

"Even after all the food I ate tonight?" Lana laughed again. "Actually, I have grown a little. That's why I'm wearing a dress without a waist. Some of my skirts and pants are already too tight to button. In another month, this pregnancy will be obvious. Just wait and see."

His hand was still on her belly. He realized that he couldn't feel the elastic band of her panties. Maybe she was wearing bikini panties. Or maybe…

Sweet Jesus, was she naked under there?

"I don't want to wait for anything." Forgetting that he should keep his distance, he cupped her behind. He didn't find elastic there either, just warm, soft flesh. "Are you wearing panties tonight? Because I sure don't feel any."

"It's a thong. That way, you don't notice a panty line through the dress."

He growled softly. "Yeah?"

"Mmm-hmm." Her pupils dilated and her lips parted in the signal he'd been waiting for.

"You drive me crazy, you know that?"

She started to say something, but before she could, he pulled her hard against his body and kissed her.

THE SPICY SCENT of Sly's aftershave filled Lana's senses and his shoulder muscles bunched under her hands. Her heart thudded so loudly, she was sure he and the entire neighborhood could hear it. Then he kissed her and everything else faded away.

Home. She was home.

All too soon, the kiss ended. He touched his forehead to hers. "I've missed this."

The silver flecks in his hot eyes seemed to glow with heat. After weeks of wanting him, Lana was in no mood to stop now. Eager to melt into another kiss, she tightened her arms around his neck. "Come back here, cowboy, and do that again."

Sly groaned and kissed her with a fierce need she felt clear to her toes. He slid his tongue across hers. He tasted of coffee and tiramisu and passion. Between her legs she grew damp and aching for him. She tried to hook her leg around his thigh but her dress was too tight. Stepping out of her sandals, she stood on his boots so that she could fit her body to his. With a sound of pure male satisfaction, he walked her backward toward the sofa. Thigh to thigh, hip to hip, his body hard in all the right places.

They sank onto the sofa, glued so tightly together they may as well have been one person. Only their clothing prevented them from joining fully. Several long, heated kisses later, Sly slid his hands to her breasts. Lana nearly moaned in relief.

He started to cup her through her dress, then hesitated. "Are you still sore?"

"Not so much." She pressed her palms to his hands, showing him what she wanted.

"Okay?" he asked.

She nodded. "That feels… Yes."

While his skilled fingers delivered dizzying pleasure

to her breasts, he kissed her neck. Somehow her skirt got hiked up and one amazing hand traveled up the inside of her bare thigh. Lana's muscles became mush, and she was glad she was sitting down.

"You have the softest skin," he murmured as his warm hand slid toward the part of her that most wanted his attention.

Lana caught her breath until finally he breached her thong. It soon disappeared. Then, oh, dear God, he touched her most sensitive spot.

Moaning in pleasure, she lifted her hips right off the sofa.

"Your passion turns me on," Sly said before he caught her in a searing kiss while his fingers drove her toward the brink.

"Sly," she gasped against his lips. "If you keep doing that, I—I'm going to…"

"Climax? That's good, Lana."

"But I…" Whatever she was planning to say faded away. She flew apart.

When she floated back to earth, he kissed her. "That was beautiful. You're beautiful."

Lana knew better. She was probably a big mess. She smoothed the skirt of her dress down, brushed her hair out of her eyes and glanced at Sly's pants. His erection was obvious.

The corners of his mouth lifted. "I'm a guy—I'm used to it. I'd better leave now while I still can."

She barely had the chance to recover before he moved away from her. "Walk me to the door?"

He stood, clasped her hands and pulled her up.

Standing in the little entry, he touched her face and kissed her again. A sweet kiss, tender and filled with promise. "Good night, Lana."

"Good night, Sly."

After locking the door behind him, she sank against it and hugged herself.

Good or bad, right or wrong, she was falling in love with Sly Pettit.

She shouldn't, and not only because of the lawsuit and her family. Sly cared for her and wanted her, but he wasn't a relationship kind of man. She would only get hurt. Then there was the baby. For his or her sake, Lana should forget about love and focus on a long-term friendship with Sly that would last.

Those arguments made a lot of sense, but her heart didn't care.

Chapter Fifteen

Monday morning, Memorial Day, Sly whistled as he met Ace, Bean and Ollie near the barn.

"You seem happy today," Ace said with a searching look. "Going to the celebration at Prosperity Park later?"

Every Memorial Day the town hosted an annual celebration and picnic at the park.

"Not this year," Sly said. He was giving his crew half the day off, but there was too much to do at the ranch for him to leave.

He should have been in a lousy mood for that and several other reasons. Ollie was still here—that was hopeful news—but he half expected the kid to ask for his paycheck and leave town at any moment. Also, Lana was pregnant, and Sly needed sex. Had needed it badly since Saturday night. But instead of going for what he wanted, he'd concentrated on Lana and drawn his own pleasure from hers.

He was still shaking his head over how good he felt about their whole evening together. So good that not even the prospect of being short one hand could bring him down. "I had a great weekend," he said.

The foreman's eyes lit with curiosity, but he didn't pry. Not that it'd have made a whit of difference. Sly wasn't going to talk about Lana.

"The wife and I went to some friend's house and played poker Saturday night," Ace said. "We beat the pants off them—won two whole dollars." He thwacked his thighs and chuckled.

Sly grinned. "What are you going to do with all that cash, Ace?"

"It went into our vacation jar, for that trip to Hawaii my wife wants."

Bean shared that he'd attended a country-and-western concert and was headed for a family picnic at the park later.

Ace glanced at Ollie, who had yet to say much. "How was your weekend, kid? Did you and that gal friend of yours go out dancing Saturday night?"

"Not this weekend." Not a hint of a smile crossed Ollie's face.

"Trouble in romance land?" Ace asked.

Ollie kicked at a hard patch of dirt that didn't budge. "I gotta talk to Sly."

"I ain't stopping you."

"Alone."

Ace held up both hands, palms out. "Sure, kid. You want to help me with that clogged irrigation pipe, Bean?"

"I'll meet you later," Sly said. When Ace and Bean disappeared from sight, he settled his hands low on his hips and studied his young ranch hand.

"I talked to Tiff." Ollie scratched the back of his neck.

"Good man. What did you two decide?"

"I guess I'll stick around for a while—if you haven't hired my replacement."

"I haven't."

Ollie nodded. It was obvious that he was finished talking.

Sly clapped his shoulder. "Let's get to work, then."

SITTING IN THE crowded waiting room of the medical clinic, Lana thumbed through a parents' magazine. There were several interesting-looking articles she wanted to read, but at the moment she was too distracted.

It was almost time for her appointment, and there was no sign of Sly. Saturday night he'd stopped by with takeout. Technically it hadn't been a date. Over dinner, Lana had reminded him about this appointment. After the meal she'd let him kiss her...and more. *Let* him? She'd made the first move. They'd stopped short of making love—she wasn't ready for that. But whenever she thought about the things she and Sly did—and she thought about them constantly—her insides went hot and soft.

Her heart was full to bursting with feelings for him. Risky, but there it was.

He didn't care as deeply for her as she did for him and probably never would, but it was obvious that he did care. And he wanted to be involved in their child's life. No matter what her own heart wanted, that was the most important thing.

Once her parents knew about the baby, she could relax. Not that telling them would change anything. Their strong belief that family loyalty stood above all else wouldn't allow them to accept Sly.

There was only one way around that obstacle. The lawsuit had to end in a way that worked for both Sly and her cousin.

As if that would ever happen.

The elevator chimed and she swung her head around. Sly exited the car. In faded jeans, cowboy boots and a chambray shirt rolled up at the cuffs, he was tall, handsome and all cowboy. As he entered the waiting room with his graceful, long-legged stride, men and women stared openly at him.

He spotted Lana, nodded and held her gaze. Her heart lifted and she forgot about her family, the lawsuit and everything else. Oh, she had it bad.

Just as he reached her, the receptionist called her name. "Lana Carpenter."

"I'll be right there," Lana replied without taking her eyes from Sly. "You made it," she said.

"Sorry to cut it so tight. I got a flat on the way here. I would have called, only I was charging my cell phone and accidentally left it at home."

They made their way to an exam room. A friendly nurse named Janet led Lana to the scale and weighed her, then jotted notes on her chart. "You gained a pound since last month. Way to go."

Sly raised his eyebrows at that.

"We like our patients to gain thirty to forty pounds over the pregnancy," Janet explained. "Two to four pounds the first trimester is ideal." She led them to an exam room, where she took Lana's pulse and blood pressure. "Everything appears normal. Dr. Valentine will be in shortly."

"How are you feeling today?" Sly asked when the nurse left.

"I was a little queasy this morning, but I'm fine now. How about you?"

"I'm doin' okay." His gaze flitted over her blouse and pants before his eyes narrowed on her legs. "What's that on your knee?"

Lana shook her head at a blob of dried paste on her leg, then wet her finger and rubbed at the spot. "We did an art project this morning. It must have—"

The knock at the door wiped the rest of her sentence from her mind. Dr. Valentine entered in her usual white lab coat and low-heeled pumps. Lana liked her doctor, who was a few years older than she was, smart and friendly.

She smiled. "Dr. Valentine, this is Sly—the baby's father."

"It's nice to meet you, Sly."

They shook hands before the ob-gyn turned to Lana. "You had your physical last month. This appointment you get to hear the fetal heartbeat."

"I can hardly wait!" Lana stole a glance at Sly. He didn't seem nearly as thrilled but he was here. That counted for something.

Dr. Valentine smiled. "This is an exciting time. Hop onto the exam table and we'll have a listen."

As soon as Lana lay down, the doctor lifted her top and positioned the sound device over her stomach. Lana heard a whooshing noise. "Is that it?"

"Not yet." Sure hands moved the device slowly over Lana's abdomen. "Right now, your baby is about the size of a tadpole, so it can be hard to find. Ah, here we are."

A rapid *thump-thump-thump* filled the room. "You're hearing your baby's heartbeat."

Overcome with emotion, Lana reached for Sly's hand.

He grasped on, a concerned expression on his face. "That sounds too fast."

"Not at all," Dr. Valentine assured him. "At this stage, one hundred and sixty beats per minute is normal for a fetus."

"Good to know." He blew out a relieved breath and squeezed Lana's hand.

For the first time ever, they were listening to their baby's heartbeat, sharing the awesome, unforgettable moment together. A look passed between them, understood only by the two of them.

"Do either of you have questions?" Dr. Valentine asked when she finished the exam.

Sly had a few that she answered before she reached for the door. "Nice meeting you, Sly. I'll see you again in a month, Lana. Be sure to stop at the front desk and schedule your appointment."

When they were alone in the little room, Sly grabbed for Lana's hand again and cleared his throat. "Now it's real."

The wonder on his face and the tender huskiness of his voice meant more than Lana could say.

Something had shifted in him, and she was now certain that he was 100 percent on board with the baby.

She realized then that she loved him.

As SLY AND Lana headed into the parking garage, feelings he didn't understand crowded his chest. Feelings that scared him, but were too powerful to push away.

Time to cut and run.

He opened his mouth to say he needed to get back to work, but something else came out instead. "I'd like to show you my ranch."

Astounded at himself, he shut his mouth. His home was his private refuge, the place where he could let go and be himself. Over the years a few women he'd dated had come to the ranch—at their own invitation, not his. But this was different. Lana was carrying his child. She ought to see the ranch.

While he was reeling from the implications of his offer, Lana dazzled him with a smile that almost brought him to his knees.

"I'd love to get the tour," she said. "Just tell me when."

Sly glanced at his watch. It was just after five. Mrs. Rutland would be on her way home and his men should be finished with the afternoon chores and relaxing in their trailers for the evening. Sly didn't want anyone who worked with him catching sight of Lana and getting ideas.

"Now works," he said. He'd quickly show her around, then send her on her way. "Why don't you follow me in your car."

"Okay. But I should warn you that I haven't eaten in several hours, and this baby likes for me to stay well fed." Laughing softly, she laid her palm over her belly. "I'm going to need food pretty soon."

Her laughter was contagious, and Sly chuckled. "Not a problem. My housekeeper makes dinner before she leaves for the day. It should be ready to heat up."

What the hell? Had he really just invited her to dinner?

"You have a cook? Lucky you."

"She cleans, too, and don't I know how lucky I am. Mrs. Rutland is the best."

Lana's happy expression faded. "There is one little problem—you live next door to Cousin Tim."

Sly frowned. "Have you ever been to the Lazy C Ranch?"

"Not since I was thirteen and my cousin was a newly-wed."

"Tim used to be married?"

"Not for long. About six months into the marriage, his wife filed for divorce and left him."

Sly hadn't been aware of that, but it explained a few things. Such as why his neighbor seemed mad at the world. Or maybe the guy had been born that way.

"Then you know that his spread is five hundred acres," he went on. "Mine is almost double that, and a fair amount of land separates our houses. You aren't likely to run into your cousin."

Lana still appeared worried. Sly figured she was having second thoughts about going to his place. Which should have been a relief but wasn't. Oddly disappointed, he shrugged. "Look, if you'd rather not…"

"No, Sly. I want to see it."

He nodded. "Then follow me."

Chapter Sixteen

As Sly turned at the black-and-white Pettit Ranch sign and rolled up the long, gravel driveway, satisfaction filled him. He'd spent a decade building his ranch into what it was today. From the freshly painted barn and outbuildings to the rolling pastures dotted with grazing cattle and horses, he was proud of it all.

He glanced in the rearview mirror. Lana trailed close behind him. He wondered if she was impressed. In a few minutes he would find out.

Just beyond the barn he signaled for her benefit, pulled over and braked to a stop. Standing beside his truck, he waited for her.

It was that magical time of day when the very air seemed bathed in oranges and pinks. Moving toward him, Lana looked unbelievably beautiful, like some woman in a painting at sunset.

Desire and those feelings Sly didn't comprehend steamrollered him. He swallowed hard. And wanted Lana gone. The sooner, the better. When she left, he would find something physically demanding to mellow him out and knock sense into his Lana-crazed brain.

"This is my ranch," he said.

If she heard any brusqueness in his voice, she didn't

let on. Wide-eyed, she took it all in. "It's huge, Sly, and beautiful—exactly what I imagine the perfect ranch to be."

His chest swelled. "Come on, I'll show you around before I put dinner in the oven."

Lana was full of questions. As Sly answered them and explained how he ran his operation, he relaxed.

Some twenty minutes later, her stomach growled. With a sheepish look, she placed her hand over her belly. "Oops."

Sly chuckled. "I'll heat up dinner."

He followed her up the front steps to the veranda that spanned the entire width of the house.

"What a great porch, and that love seat seems cozy," Lana said. "I want to curl up there with a good book."

Sly nodded. "It's a swing, too, and one of my favorite places to sit in the evening, after the chores are done."

Lately he'd sat out here a lot at night, working on just how he was going to fit his kid into his life without screwing up.

Lana glanced upward. "This house is huge—at least twice the size of my town house."

Too big for one person, but Sly had had nothing to do with that. "The people I bought it from had three kids. I guess they needed the room."

"What happened to them?"

"The bank was getting ready to foreclose on the property, and they wanted out."

"That's too bad."

"Ranching isn't easy, and they were relieved to trade this life for one in the city. Last I heard, they were doing okay." He opened the front door and gestured Lana inside.

As she stepped into the vestibule, Sly couldn't help but picture her and their child here, filling the house with noise and laughter.

That stopped him. No way, no how. He enjoyed living alone.

Cursing himself for inviting Lana over, he turned away from her questioning gaze. "This way," he said with a curt nod.

She fell into step beside him.

"I envy you all the space in here," she said as she entered the kitchen.

It was big, all right, with room enough for a small horde. Usually Sly and Mrs. Rutland were the only ones in here, with periodic visits from Dani and an occasional crew member.

Having Lana in here felt…different. Felt right. Frowning, Sly switched on the oven.

"What can I do to help?" she asked.

Go home, he thought, *before I do something we'll both regret.* But it was too late for that. She'd already agreed to eat with him.

She gave him one of the smiles that erased his common sense. Hell, who was he kidding? As bad an idea as bringing her to the ranch was, he definitely wanted her here. He wanted her, period.

"Sly?" Lana was shooting him a funny look. "I asked if there's something I can do to help with dinner."

"How about setting the table."

After Lana washed her hands, he showed her where to find the place mats and utensils.

As she bent down to arrange them out on the table, she kicked the ordinary task to a whole new level of hot.

He really was losing it. Tired of his one-track mind, Sly grabbed two glasses from the cabinet. "While dinner heats, I'll give you the five-cent house tour."

He showed her the main floor—living room, den, dining and powder rooms.

"All the bedrooms are upstairs?" she asked.

"That's right—all four of them."

Her sudden, telltale blush revealed that she was thinking about all the beds in those rooms, just as he was. But inviting her, or any woman, to bed at his house was off-limits.

And yet he considered breaking his rule just this once, and giving her a hands-on tour of his king-size bed.

The oven buzzed and Sly jerked his thoughts back to the here and now. His brain heaved a relieved sigh, but his body wasn't happy.

The sooner Lana left, the better.

"Time to eat," he said, and they returned to the kitchen.

Sly didn't say much as Lana sat down at his kitchen table. Without so much as a "help yourself," he silently passed her a steaming casserole that smelled amazing.

He seemed ill at ease, but so was she. For some reason, sharing the evening meal at his ranch table felt like a big step.

Too big for a man who wasn't into relationships.

Plus, whether he wanted to be or not, they were on the verge of the relationship of their lives—parenting their child. It would be a huge change they both needed time to adjust to.

Wanting to ease the tension, Lana smiled. "This is delicious. Please thank your housekeeper for me."

"Will do."

Sly didn't say another word, and for a while the only sounds were their cutlery against the plates.

She tried again. "What would you be doing if I weren't here right now?"

"Probably eating in front of the tube."

"Sometimes I do that, too, or I read the paper." Better either of those than focusing on the loneliness of eating alone. "And occasionally I work while I eat."

"Not me. I pay bills and do any paperwork *after* the meal. Less indigestion that way."

He seemed more at ease now. Lana relaxed, too. "My parents would agree with you," she said. "When my sister and I were kids, they insisted on no television or phone calls during dinner. We tried to eat together every night, but once Liz and I started high school, we both had so many after-school activities that family dinners were hard to manage."

"What kinds of activities?"

"Liz played soccer and joined the swim team, and I worked on the yearbook and the sets for our school plays."

Sly actually smiled. "With your artistic skills, I can picture you painting scenery."

"That's exactly what I did. What about you, Sly?" Lana asked. "What sorts of activities were you involved in?"

"Like your sister, I was into sports. Football, baseball. That's how I was able to attend college—on a baseball scholarship."

"No kidding." She'd never have guessed. There was so much she didn't know about Sly. "Did you ever consider going pro?"

"Sure. I figured I'd do that after high school. Then my coach took me aside and convinced me to get a college education instead. And he was right. As it turned out, I was an okay ballplayer, but not good enough for the pros."

"I used to think I wanted to go to New York and be a set designer for one of the theaters—maybe even Broadway," Lana said. "Then in college I took a couple of child psychology courses and decided I wanted a career that involved kids."

"You made the right choice," Sly said.

"Seems that we both did."

"For me it was pure luck. The scholarship covered tuition, but I still needed money for books, room and board. I told you about finding work at a ranch, and here I am."

Lana nodded. "When I was little, I begged my parents to buy a ranch so we could live there. But they saw how hard my great-uncle Horace struggled to make ends meet. They didn't want that. Cousin Tim inherited the Lazy C from Horace."

"Dealing with Mother Nature and crop prices is always a struggle," Sly said. "But the work is rewarding. I enjoy it."

His face was lit up now. Lana smiled to herself. "How did you come to own all this?"

"The rancher who hired me, a guy named Bill Hodges, respected my work ethic. When he asked me what I wanted to do with my life, I said I wanted to own a successful ranch like his. He took me under his wing and mentored me just as a father would a son."

Sly sat back and stared into space a moment, as if remembering. "With his help, I was able to purchase a small spread north of town. A couple of years later, the state bought my land for that new freeway. I netted enough to buy this place."

Lana was impressed. "Are you still in contact with Mr. Hodges?"

Glancing down, Sly shook his head. "A year after I bought this place, he passed away."

He'd lost so many people he cared about. Lana's heart ached for him. "That's a shame. He'd be so proud of you now."

"I like to think so. My turn to ask the questions. Did you have any serious boyfriends in high school and college?"

"A couple of boyfriends, but nothing that lasted. Brent was my first real relationship. We met just before we graduated from college and dated almost three years before we got married."

Then four years of marriage and another eighteen months mourning the breakup… With a shock, Lana realized she'd spent eight and a half years of her life focused on Brent. And she had nothing to show for those years, except that she was sadder, wiser and older. She counted herself lucky to be free of him.

Otherwise she wouldn't be pregnant now.

She touched her belly and smiled. "I'll bet you had lots of girlfriends."

"A few."

"Anyone serious?"

"There was one girl I was serious about in college."

His somber expression made her curious. "What happened?"

"We talked about marriage, but her parents disapproved of me. I was a kid from a broken home and not good enough for their precious daughter. I didn't even own a suit, and that was real important to them. Apparently she decided they were right—she broke up with me." He gave a dismissive shrug.

"Ouch. But a broken home? Your parents died."

"True, but it was more that I didn't have two dimes to rub together, and they didn't think I ever would."

Indignant on Sly's behalf, Lana scoffed. "There are lots of college kids who start off poor and end up doing really well. You did. Those people were total snobs."

"Hey, it was a long time ago. I got over it." Sly glanced

down at his work shirt and faded jeans. His mouth quirked. "If they could only see me now."

The meal was winding down. Soon Sly could plead fatigue or evening chores and send Lana home. It was what he should have wanted. And yet he lingered at the table.

Lana slanted her head his way. "A nickel for your thoughts."

Tonight he'd revealed more about himself than most people ever knew. Not just because she'd asked, but because she cared. A lot—too much. Usually when that happened, Sly felt hemmed in by a relationship and wanted out. He wasn't about to analyze why this time felt different.

"I was considering asking you to help me clean up this mess," he teased.

Lana arched her eyebrows. "That depends, Mr. Pettit, on whether you're planning to bribe me with the brownies over there on the counter."

"Mrs. R made them, and they're killer. Help me with the dishes and you can have as many as you want."

"For brownies, I'll do just about anything."

"Anything?" he drawled, letting his gaze rove slowly over her.

In the silence, desire hung between them in the suddenly thick air.

Lana shifted restlessly in her seat, the sudden blush on her face and hunger in her eyes burning him like a heated caress.

His body throbbed to life. He had a fair idea what Lana wanted tonight, but he wasn't going there—not here. If they'd been at her place, sure. But at his ranch, in his bed? No way.

He cleared his throat and stood. "Let's get this done."

Fifteen minutes later the leftovers had been stowed in

the fridge, the kitchen was clean and Sly had managed to corral his randy libido.

With a smile tugging her lips, Lana held out her hand. "I'll take that bribe now."

Sly pulled the plastic wrap from the brownie plate. "It's a nice evening," he said. "Let's have our dessert outside."

Where the air between them was bound to be cooler.

On the porch, Lana plunked down on the swing. His swing.

Sly grabbed a brownie for himself, passed the plate to her and then bypassed several porch chairs to sit on the top step, a good five feet from her. Able to breathe better now, he sucked in the fresh air.

Lana frowned. "Why are you sitting all the way over there on the hard steps when you could be sitting in a chair or sharing this nice, padded swing with me? And hey, in case you didn't realize, you can't trust me with these brownies."

Trust. A rarity in his life. She'd always been straight with him and he sensed that she always would be.

Which explained why, against his better judgment, he *was* beginning to trust her.

He hadn't wanted to do that—trusting someone only led to pain.

"I don't bite, you know," she added when he remained silent.

Oh, he knew. He was about to ask her to leave when she spoke.

"I think I'll have another brownie. They're so delicious, I just might finish them all. Then I'll get sick, and it'll be your fault for not helping me eat them."

"Those things are really rich," he said. "You'll never be able to eat the whole plate."

"I'm pregnant, remember?"

"You drive a hard bargain."

"That's what people tell me." She patted the seat beside her and smiled serenely.

Sly gave up. "All right." He ambled over and sat down, keeping the brownie plate between them.

They ate and chatted about this and that, both of them pushing the rocker back and forth in the growing darkness. It would have been really comfortable if a certain part of Sly's body wasn't primed and ready for action.

Down, boy, he ordered it. Not here and not tonight.

"Now that we've heard the baby's heartbeat, I'm ready to say something to Liz and Eric about pregnancy," Lana said. "If it's okay with you, I'm thinking I'll do it after work tomorrow."

That she was checking with him first sat well in his chest. "Sure," he said. "I'll tell Dani then, too."

There was one brownie left. Sly was eyeing it when Lana divided it and handed him half.

"What about your parents?" he asked as he polished it off. "When are you planning to give them the news?"

Lana had been about to eat her brownie. Now she bit her lip and set it down again. "Liz and Eric will be excited and happy for me. If I know my sister, it won't be easy for her to keep something this big to herself. Especially from our mom and dad. I should tell them right after I tell her." She let out a heavy sigh. "I dread that."

"If family is as important to them as you say, they'll support you no matter what."

"I'm not so sure about that." She offered a weak smile.

"Because I'm the father and I'm suing dear old Cousin Tim."

She nodded.

Sly swore. No matter how carefully he examined the situation, there was no easy way out. No out, period.

Neither of them spoke after that. The swing creaked as he pushed it with his foot. In the distance, an owl hooted.

"Know what I like about you?" he said after a while.

"My ability to consume vast quantities of sweets?"

"That, and the fact that no matter what, you're always straight with me."

"I'm not wired to hold in my thoughts."

"Except when it comes to sharing them with your parents."

"I want to get along with them."

Her beautiful eyes pleaded with him to understand, and he lost himself in them. "I'll come with you when you tell them," he offered.

She glanced away and her hands started their fidget routine, a sure sign that something was bothering her. "I don't know, Sly. That probably isn't such a great idea."

"They can hate me all they want. You're carrying my baby, and you don't want to face them alone. I want to be there with you."

"You'd do that for me? You're a good man, Sly Pettit. I'm awful glad my baby will have you for a daddy."

Her warmth and sincerity went straight to his heart. She stroked his cheek, then leaned across the plate, cupped his face in her hands and kissed him. Nothing passionate, a light brush of her lips against his. But her sweetness was there, tempting him like a siren's song.

Fighting a losing battle to control his desire, and forgetting that on his ranch he wanted to keep his distance, he caught hold of her hand and kissed the sensitive inside of her wrist.

He heard her swallow and felt her pulse bump against his mouth, pounding almost has hard as his heart.

The brownie plate clattered onto the porch planking, a loud warning that what he was about to do was a bad idea.

"Oops," Lana murmured, her voice husky with desire. "There goes the dessert plate." Her lips parted, her eyelids lowered and she wrapped her arms around his neck.

Need roared through him, crushing the last of his tenuous grip on his control. He pulled her onto his lap and gave in.

Chapter Seventeen

Sly's mouth was hard, demanding. Weak with desire, Lana sank against him. Her mind blanked and her whole world shrank to just her and him, slowly rocking in the cooling night air. Hours later, or maybe it was only a few minutes, Sly pulled away.

His breathing was labored, as if he'd just sprinted a quarter mile. "If we don't stop now, Lana, I won't be able to."

"I don't want to stop," she whispered. She tried to kiss him again, but to her frustration, he lifted her off his lap and deposited her on her side of the swing.

"You've been saying you're not ready."

"I am now."

"It won't hurt the baby?"

Lana shook her head.

"You're sure you want to do this?"

Lana had never been more certain. Without hesitation, she nodded.

Sly's exhale sounded like pure relief. "First we have to get a few things straight."

"Let me guess what you're going to say—you're not into relationships," she ventured.

"Right. I like you, and I want to be part of your life while we raise our kid." He glanced at his erection. "It's obvious that I want to be with you sexually. But my feelings about a committed relationship haven't changed."

What he'd described sounded like a committed relationship to Lana, but just now she was too impatient to quibble over definitions. "Got it," she said. "Now, please, take me to bed."

Sly hesitated, searching her face a moment, before he grasped her hand, tugged her to her feet and pulled her inside.

FOREPLAY WAS SLY'S second favorite part of lovemaking. He enjoyed taking his time, but with Lana molded to him and kissing him hotly on the way upstairs, that proved challenging. Her passion and enthusiasm scorched him and nearly sent him over the edge. Halfway up, he lifted her into his arms and carried her the rest of the way.

"Mmm, you're carrying me. Why?" she asked in a sexy voice that thrilled him.

"I want to make sure we reach the bedroom while I still can."

Moments later he set her down. Standing a few feet in front of him with her gaze locked on his, she slowly removed her top. Her skin was flushed with desire. She wore a lacy black bra she almost spilled out of, and her taut nipples were clearly visible.

"Now you," she said.

She didn't have to ask twice. Sly unbuttoned a few buttons of his shirt, then pulled the thing over his head.

They shed their pants at the same time. Then he was down to his shorts, and she… In a black bra and a matching pair of bikini panties, she looked sexy as hell. So beautiful.

His.

Sly swallowed. "As much as I like your underwear, it has to go."

With a seductive look, Lana reached behind her and un-hooked the clasp. The bra dropped to the floor.

"Now I can see the changes in your body. Your breasts are bigger." He cupped her reverently in his hands. "Heavier."

Lana's eyelids drifted down.

"Your nipples are darker." Aware of her sensitivity, he lightly traced each rigid tip with his finger, pleased when she shivered.

Continuing his study of her, he placed his palm over her belly, just as he'd watched her do to herself countless times. "Your stomach is slightly rounded."

"Y-yes," she replied, as if talking were difficult. "Does that bother you?"

Sly shook his head. "You're perfect." He let his fingers trail lower. "Warm, too, and smooth."

He reached the elastic band in her panties. As he dis-posed of them, Lana sucked in a breath.

"You're incredibly responsive," he said, slipping his fin-ger inside her. "It's hot."

"It's you, Sly. What you're doing now... I don't think my legs will support me any longer."

"Don't worry, I've got you." He lifted her off the ground and gently deposited her on the bed. "Now, where were we?" He parted her folds. "This part hasn't changed at all. But maybe I should check more closely."

Lana tensed. He tasted her most sensitive place, enjoy-ing her gasps of pleasure.

In no time, she shifted restlessly and moaned. Moments later, she let go and shattered.

After recovering she gave him a wicked smile. "Your turn, cowboy. On your back."

With her blond hair every which way and her proud breasts heaving, she straddled his thighs. His very own, very hot goddess. She wrapped her hand around his arousal. Sly saw stars. He stopped her before he lost control.

Lana frowned at him. "Hey, I was just getting started."

"I don't want to finish without you. Understand?"

Still on his back, he positioned her where he needed her. One thrust and he was deep inside her, exactly where he wanted to be.

Shuddering with desire, Lana contracted her muscles and squeezed him. Heat and pleasure roared through Sly, and he forgot about taking it slow. Gripping her hips, he thrust upward. Harder and faster and deeper, until he was mindless with need. Lana cried out and together they spiraled out of control.

When he finally came down to earth again, she lay sprawled across his chest, her head tucked under his chin. Spent and utterly sated, he held her close. "Wow," he said. "That was even better than I remembered."

She raised her head and smiled at him with lips that were swollen from the deep kisses they'd shared. "It was pretty amazing."

Keeping his arm around her, he rolled her to his side. After a while Lana's breathing evened out. Sly figured she'd fallen asleep.

Feeling tender and protective, he pulled the covers up over her shoulders. Lana mumbled and burrowed closer.

Sly felt unbelievable. Great. Complete.

Hold the fort. He didn't want these emotions, couldn't take the risk of caring too much.

She could leave him, and as with most everyone else he'd ever cared about, probably would. That scared him even more than his overpowering feelings for her.

As he started to untangle his limbs from hers, his groin accidentally brushed against her hand.

Just like that, he was hard again. He slid his palm over

her bottom, then between her legs. Her breath caught in the aroused little sound he'd come to anticipate.

They began to make love again, and for a long time Sly didn't have a single coherent thought.

MUCH LATER, AFTER enjoying the best sex of his life—twice—Sly lay on his back with one arm under his head and the other around Lana.

It was going to take a while to recover. Then she kissed his rib cage with her soft, warm lips. As spent as he was, his body stirred and he wanted her all over again.

God help him, he couldn't get enough of her, and didn't think he ever would. While he debated how to deal with that, she propped herself on her elbows.

"I never knew it could be like this," she said, staring at him as if he were something special.

"We have great chemistry."

"It's more than that. When we make love, you're so considerate and caring."

"Are you saying your previous lovers weren't—not even your ex?"

"Let's just say that Brent was more into his own satisfaction than mine."

Sly didn't understand guys like that. "He didn't deserve you. You were right to divorce him."

"*He* divorced *me*," she corrected in the straightforward way he admired. "I was hurt and it took me a while to move on. But I can't say I'm sorry about the divorce. Because if Brent and I had stayed together—" she planted a sweet kiss on Sly's chest "—I wouldn't be here now with you."

It was about as close to a declaration of love as she could get without saying the words. Sly wasn't ready for that, but she knew the score. She kissed his rib cage, then his belly. His mind blanked.

He was tasting his way down her body when her stomach growled. Loudly.

Chuckling, he gave up. "I guess it's time to feed you again."

Lana smiled and shrugged. "Apparently."

They were in the kitchen, foraging through the fridge, when the first bars of "Mama Knows" filled the air. "Is that your cell phone?" Sly asked.

Lana straightened and turned away from the fridge. She was wearing one of his clean T-shirts. It almost swallowed her up. Sly liked that.

"Yep. It's my mother—the last person I want to talk to. It's almost ten-thirty. She's usually in bed by now." She shot Sly a panicked look. "What if something's happened?"

"Maybe you should answer it."

"Talk to my mom right after you and I had sex?"

"She won't know that. This might be a good time to mention me," he suggested.

He saw right away she wasn't ready for that conversation. "Tell her some other time, then," he said. "Listen, I haven't checked my phone since I left here before your doctor's appointment. I'll do that while you talk to her."

Before Lana answered her cell phone, she sat down at the kitchen table. Sly was standing at the counter, listening to his messages. Shirtless and barefoot, with the top button of his jeans undone, he looked like a walking ad for sex appeal—except for the stunned expression on his face. Lana was so curious about that, she almost ignored her chirping phone.

She answered just as Sly disconnected and joined her at the table.

"Hi, Mom," she said, rolling her eyes at him. "You're calling so late. Is everything okay?"

"Yes, fine."

"That's a relief." Lana let out a sigh. "I'm sort of busy right now. Can I call you back in the morning?"

"Let me guess—you're online, visiting that adoption site again, hoping to find a pregnant girl who wants her baby to go to a single mother."

If that wasn't the beginning of a lecture... Lana was relieved she'd never told her mother about Sophie, and anxious to get her mother off the phone. "No internet for me tonight," she said. "This is something completely different." She smiled at Sly.

His solemn expression puzzled her.

"Well, it must be important," her mother said, sounding out of sorts. "In the past hour, I've called you twice. Both times I had to leave a message. I'm glad you finally decided you could spare a moment to talk to me."

"Way to guilt-trip me, Mom. I, uh, left my phone in the kitchen, and didn't hear it ring before."

Which was true. Her phone had been in her purse, which she'd placed on the counter. "You're usually asleep by now. Whatever you have to say must be important."

"It is. Your father and I heard from Cousin Tim earlier and I have some interesting news. He's decided to countersue Mr. Pettit."

Lana's jaw dropped. "Cousin Tim is countersuing Sly... er, Mr. Pettit?" she repeated for Sly's benefit.

She saw by his grim expression that he'd already heard. He pointed at his phone. Someone must have left him a message about it.

"That's right," her mother said. "It seems a few of Cousin Tim's cows have turned up sick. One even died. He's claiming that Sly Pettit poisoned them."

Sly wouldn't do that. Or would he? Of course not, Lana assured herself. Yet she distinctly remembered what Sly had said that night at the Italian restaurant. That he was tired of waiting for the lawsuit to settle and that he wished he could do something to push it along.

Was this was his way of righting the wrongs he believed her cousin had done?

Doubts crept in, unwanted but impossible to ignore. As Lana met Sly's gaze, she suddenly felt sick.

In a blink, his eyes lost all warmth. His entire expression shuttered and closed, almost as if he'd read her mind.

Without a word, he stood and spun away from her, his shoulders set and his spine stiff. Lana realized that somehow he'd sensed her suspicion.

He opened the back door, walked out and shut it behind him with a firm click.

Her mother was saying something about Cousin Tim, but Lana couldn't focus. "I have to go," she said.

She disconnected and then headed outside to find Sly.

Chapter Eighteen

Sly was still reeling from Dave Swain's message. Tim Carpenter's accusations and countersuit—all of it was a big load of bull crap, stuff he would deal with when he contacted the attorney in the morning.

What he couldn't handle was Lana's off-the-cuff gut reaction to the news. Her expression had clearly revealed that she suspected he'd poisoned Carpenter's cattle.

That stung and made him mad, too. Mostly at himself for breaking his own cardinal rule and trusting her. And for starting to care.

What a damn fool he was. He wanted to head for the barn, jump on Bee and gallop through the darkness until his mind emptied. But he needed his boots for that, and they were in his bedroom. Sly wasn't about to return to the house until he pulled himself together.

And so he paced the porch in his bare feet. The motion-activated lights kicked on, and he could easily see where he was going. Step around the furniture. *Thud-thud-thud.* Pivot around and don't think. *Thud-thud-thud.*

He was starting his third lap and nowhere near calm when the back door opened and Lana slipped outside. Light from the kitchen sliced right through the T-shirt he'd loaned her, silhouetting her naked body. The body he lusted after and couldn't get enough of.

Even now, smarting and angry, he wanted her. Sly called himself every name in the book—idiot, lamebrain, stupid jerk and a few four-letter epithets he wouldn't use on his worst enemy.

Lana reached out to him. "Please, can we talk?"

"What for?" He stepped away from her. "You assume I poisoned those cows."

On the slim hope that he'd misread her, he sucked in a breath and waited for her to deny it. She didn't.

His laugh sounded hollow even to his own ears. "You should leave," he said.

"Not like this."

"That's right—you're wearing my shirt. Go upstairs and get your clothes."

"That's not what I meant, Sly, and you know it. If you want me to go, I will, but not while you're angry. First we have to straighten this out."

"You should have thought about that before you assumed I poisoned your cousin's cows."

Barefoot or not, if he didn't get some space, he'd explode. He strode down the porch steps and kept going, wincing as he stepped on pebbles and God knew what else, until he heard the kitchen door close as Lana reentered the house.

Before long she was outside again, in her own clothes, purse slung over her shoulder and keys in hand. She stopped right in front of him, just beyond the reach of the porch light. Even so, he could see the gleam of her pleading eyes.

"You wouldn't poison anyone's cattle," she said. "Neither would Cousin Tim. I just… His countersuit caught me by surprise."

Nothing she said explained the shock and horror on her face when her mother had told her what had happened. That Lana had suspected him, even for a moment, was unacceptable. Unbearable.

Sly's heart constricted painfully. He had trusted her, but she couldn't trust him. He gave a terse nod. "Good night, Lana."

Her mouth trembled, and for a minute he feared she was going to cry. God above, he hoped not. He was already treading on thin emotional ice himself, hurt to the quick and barely holding it together.

But she only raised her chin and walked past him, into the darkness and toward her car.

SLY WOKE UP Wednesday in a bum mood, and things only got worse after he spoke with his attorney. "I didn't do it," he told Dave.

"I know that, Sly."

His attorney believed in him. Why couldn't Lana?

He was still kicking himself for letting his guard down last night. For allowing her to get too close.

"The question is, can you prove it to Tim Carpenter?" his attorney asked.

"How the hell am I supposed to prove I didn't do it?" Sly grumbled. "I assume he had an autopsy done on the animal that died."

"He used the same vet as you. His heifer had arsenic poisoning. The three that are sick have the same symptoms, but they'll probably survive."

"Sounds very similar to what happened to my cattle," Sly said. "Carpenter must think I'm retaliating for what he did. Oh, that's rich. What am I supposed to do now?"

"My suggestion is for you and Tim Carpenter to work with a mediation attorney. I can recommend one who's top-notch. I spoke with him earlier and he's willing to work with the two of you to reach some kind of resolution."

"There's nothing to resolve," Sly said. "I didn't do it."

"As you know all too well, Tim Carpenter is claiming the same thing."

Sly mumbled a few choice words and for the first time, considered a new angle. What if someone else was involved? "Let me think about the mediator and get back to you."

He spent most of the next two days alone on his horse, galloping across the ranch in search of calves that had become separated from the herd. He didn't find any. Which was a good thing, but Sly needed the distraction that herding a lost calf or two would have provided. With effort he managed to steer his mind away from Lana and their night together. That had become too painful to remember.

Instead, he focused on the new turn of events with Carpenter. Before the countersuit, he'd believed the situation was as bad as it could get. He'd been wrong. His life seemed to be spinning out of control.

The poisonings were too similar to be a coincidence, which meant someone was messing with them. But if another person was involved, how would Sly ever recoup the money he'd lost, and how could he possibly find that person?

Late Friday morning he made a decision. He couldn't go on like this, and he hoped Carpenter felt the same. He would attempt to talk to his neighbor again, so that they could straighten out this mess. Just the two of them, without a mediator or any lawyers involved.

His mind made up, he rode Bee to her favorite pasture, removed her saddle and slapped her lightly on the rump. She trotted to a big shady hawthorn and began to nibble sweet grass. Sly slid his cell phone from his pocket. He was searching for Carpenter's number when his own cell phone rang.

The screen identified the caller as Timothy Carpenter.

Speak of the devil. "Carpenter," Sly said by way of greeting. "I was just about to call you."

"Were you, now. Planning on cussing me out?"

"Something like that. You and I need to sit down and talk. No lawyers—just you and me, man-to-man."

"Damn straight, we do."

That the rancher was willing to talk with Sly at all was progress of a sort. "Where and when?" Sly asked.

"My place. Now."

"As long as you don't point any guns at me or try to take a punch at me."

"I won't, if you don't accuse me of something I didn't do."

"No guns, no accusations," Sly agreed. "Just the two of us talking things through."

Fifteen minutes later he drove up Carpenter's driveway, past a barn that had seen better days. He stopped next to the house, which could use a coat or two of paint. The buildings at the Lazy C needed work, but the fields beyond were green and populated with livestock. Sly noted a tractor and a few men in the distance.

His neighbor was standing on the porch, wearing reflector sunglasses and a Stetson. As Sly crossed the yard, Carpenter folded his arms over his chest.

Matching his unwelcoming scowl, Sly climbed the stairs. Neither of them removed their hats or their sunglasses. "I didn't poison your cattle," he stated.

"Yeah? Well, I didn't poison yours, either."

Though Carpenter had five or six years on Sly, they were roughly the same height and both muscular and strong. Despite the sunglasses, Sly sensed his hostile glare.

He rested his hands low on his hips. "You gonna ask me to sit down, or are we going to do this standing up?"

His neighbor nodded at a pair of lawn chairs in the front

yard, in the shade of an old black walnut. They both sat down, their weight causing the old chairs to creak.

"I'd have bet my left arm that you poisoned my cows to get back at me for dragging out the lawsuit," Carpenter said.

Sly snorted. "That's not how I work. Ask anyone in town. I prefer to solve my problems by talking them out."

The ones that weren't too personal, that was. He tended to keep those close to the chest. "I'm starting to wonder if someone else might have set us both up."

Carpenter bent down and plucked a blade of grass, the expression of doubt on his face reminding Sly of Lana.

That she believed him capable of poisoning Carpenter's cows hurt. But he didn't want to think about that. Pushing the pain inside, he waited his neighbor out.

Carpenter straightened again, stuck the blade of grass between his lips and rolled it to the corner of his mouth before he went on. "You're smarter than you look, Pettit. Something came to my attention this morning that put me of the same mind."

Sly tipped his hat back and pulled off his shades. "What are you saying?"

Carpenter, too, removed his sunglasses and met Sly's gaze. "That someone who wanted to do me serious harm set me up by poisoning your cattle and making me look guilty. When things didn't go as fast as he wanted, he upped the ante and poisoned some of mine."

Sly swore. "You must have made some nasty enemies." Given Carpenter's sour disposition, not hard to believe. "Just who is this crazy person?"

"A son of a dog by the name of Pitch Alberts."

Sly had never heard of the man. "I'm not familiar with him."

"You wouldn't be. About a year and half ago he came into town looking for a job. He worked for me until mid-

November of last year. That's when I found out he was stealing hay and cattle feed from me. Of course, I sacked him. He didn't have any money. I knew he'd never pay me back for what he'd stolen, and the loss wasn't big enough for me to press charges.

"Pitch didn't appreciate losing his job just before the holidays, but that was his fault. I told him he was lucky I didn't call the sheriff."

Sly probably would have done the same thing as Carpenter.

"Pitch hadn't crossed my mind since, until Eddie, a guy on my summer crew, said he ran into Pitch last night at a bar. Pitch had had a few and was bragging that he'd fixed my wagon. From there it was a matter of putting two and two together."

Sly shook his head. "I trust you've been in touch with Sheriff Dean."

"This morning, right after Eddie told me. Sheriff Dean's been out searching for Pitch, to take him in for questioning. As yet, that's all I know, but I'd stake my ranch that he did it."

"If that's true, then I owe you an apology," Sly said.

"I'll take it. I'll owe you one, too. By the way, my lawyer advised me to keep all this to myself for now. I wouldn't want Pitch suing me for slander." The corner of Carpenter's mouth lifted, the closest he'd ever come to smiling.

"Copy that. I'll do the same, then. Keep me informed."

"After my lawyer, you'll be the first person I'll contact."

They shook hands and parted almost amicably, Sly in a much better mood than when he'd arrived. Things hadn't turned out at all as he'd expected, and he shook his head at that.

Regardless, he still needed the new drainage system, and he still didn't want to borrow money to pay for it. He'd been so focused on either getting reimbursed by Carpenter or taking out a costly loan that he hadn't considered other options. There had to be another way.

His mind spinning, he returned home. Sitting in the truck in his driveway, he phoned Dave and filled him in. "I'll keep you updated," he promised.

Then he contacted Bob Haggerty, the engineer who owned the drainage-system company, and set up a meeting for later that afternoon.

It was a relief to have the answers to all the questions he'd had for months now. Lana would want to know what had happened, and Sly itched to fill her in. But he and Carpenter had agreed to keep it quiet for now. Besides, after the other night, Sly wouldn't be telling her anything.

His high spirits nose-dived and his chest constricted. He felt as if he was suffocating. If not for a recent physical and the news that he was as fit as a kid half his age, he'd have called his doctor.

There was just time to fit in a ride on Bee before the meeting with Haggerty. Sly stalked toward the pasture and whistled for his horse. He rode her bareback, racing into the wind until finally his mind cleared and he could breathe again.

OVER THE PAST few days, Lana had tried to act as if she was fine and nothing had changed. Apparently she sucked at faking happiness. Jasmine and Brittany tiptoed around her with sympathetic expressions, and even the most rambunctious kids had behaved.

By Friday she was a basket case, in need of a friendly ear. After a quick SOS to Kate, she went directly from work to her friend's apartment for pizza and sympathy.

"The pizza should be here soon," Kate said when she let Lana in. "Sit down and tell me what's wrong."

Out of habit, Lana placed her hand over her stomach, but even the beloved child growing inside failed to bring her comfort.

Kate's eyes widened a fraction before she gave Lana a stricken look. "You're okay, right?"

"The baby is fine," Lana assured her, and counted her blessings that at least that part of her life was going well.

"That's good." Her friend blew out a big breath. "So what's the matter?"

Where to begin? "For starters, I'm in love with Sly."

"That's obvious. He wants to be part of the baby's life, right? He even showed up at your doctor's appointment the other day. You can't ask for more than that from a commitmentphobe. We haven't touched base since before the appointment. How did it go?"

"Great. Sly and I got along so well that after the doctor's appointment, he invited me to his ranch and showed me around. He fed me dinner, too. He doesn't do that with just anyone."

"No wonder we haven't talked all week. Sounds to me as if Mr. Single is getting serious. Go on."

"We had sex."

Kate gave her a funny look. "He disappointed you?"

Lana shook her head. "Sly is the best lover I've ever had."

"Lucky you," Kate said. "That sounds pretty darned perfect. So what's the problem?"

"Everything was wonderful—then my mother phoned."

"You answered her call when you were with Sly? Are you nuts?"

"I'm beginning to think I might be." Lana gnawed on her thumbnail...or what was left of it. "We were in the kitchen, grabbing a snack." They'd been happy and relaxed. "It was later than she usually calls, and I was worried."

Lana wished she could go back in time and switch off her phone, or at least ignore the call. Unfortunately, that was impossible. "It wasn't an emergency. She wanted to tell me that someone had poisoned Cousin Tim's cows. One even died. My cousin is blaming Sly and countersuing."

"No." Kate's jaw dropped. "Sly would never do anything like that!"

Lana envied her friend's instant certainty. If she'd reacted with the same outrage, Tuesday night would have ended very differently.

"That's a pretty sad face you're making," Kate commented. "Things can't be that bad."

"You haven't heard the whole story yet." Lana's head hurt. She massaged her temples. "I really screwed up, Kate. When I heard about the poisoning, I couldn't help but wonder whether Sly had done it."

"After all the great things you've said about him, you really believe he'd do something like that?"

"Not in my heart. It was sort of a gut reaction."

Kate just shook her head. "And you said this to Sly?"

"I didn't have to. He saw my face, and you know what an open book that is." Dropping her head to her hands, Lana groaned. "It was horrible of me to suspect him, even for a moment."

Wonderful friend that Kate was, she didn't comment, she just sat quietly and waited for Lana to pour out the rest of the miserable story.

Lana gave her all the awful details. "I'd do anything to change those seconds of doubt," she concluded. "I wish there was a way that I could convince Sly that I believe in him, and that I'm absolutely certain he would never do what my cousin is accusing him of."

"I think you should tell Sly what you just told me. If he's as good a man as you claim, he's bound to forgive you."

"You weren't there. The way he looked at me..." With shuttered eyes and a cool disdain, as if he were seeing her for the first time and didn't like the woman he saw.

Lana wanted to sob. "Trust doesn't come easy to him, but I'm pretty sure he was beginning to trust me. And I blew everything by not trusting *him*. I hurt him, Kate." She hung her head. "I lost my chance with him."

Now Kate became glum, too. "There must be something you can do."

For the life of her, Lana couldn't come up with anything. "Like what?"

"Well..." Kate tapped her finger to her lips and appeared pensive. "Invite him over and cook his favorite foods. Then apologize and swear you'll always believe in him."

"He's angry at me. I doubt he'd come. Besides, words and a meal wouldn't prove anything. It has to be something important." An idea popped into her mind that she needed to test on Kate. "What if I go to my parents' house right now and tell them about Sly? Then I could drive over to Cousin Tim's and convince him that Sly would never hurt his animals."

"Great idea," Kate said. "It's about time your parents knew about Sly. As for your cousin, he doesn't strike me as a man easily swayed by anyone else's opinion. How will Sly even know that you went to bat for him?"

Lana wasn't about to let that stop her. "I'll pound on Sly's door and make him listen. If I want a chance with him, I have to restore his trust in me, and prove that I trust him."

"Wow, lady, you're on fire." Kate thought a moment. "I hate to bring this up, but what if it doesn't work?"

Refusing to consider the possibility, Lana raised her chin. "It will. It has to." She reached for her purse and stood.

"Now?" Kate frowned. "But what about the pizza?"

"Eat a piece for me. This won't wait."

Chapter Nineteen

As Lana rode the elevator down from Kate's fourth-floor apartment, "Mama Knows" sounded from her cell phone.

She picked up right away. "Hi. I'm glad you called." She could almost hear her mother's surprise at that. "I'm on my way over to the house now. I have something important to tell you and Dad. I'll be there shortly." Before her mother had a chance to question Lana, she disconnected.

She wasn't going to reveal her pregnancy to her parents just yet—one step at a time. Besides, she wanted to tell Liz and Eric first. Tonight was about Sly.

Thanks to the usual Friday rush-hour traffic, she didn't pull up to her parents' house for a good twenty minutes. Which gave her way too long to imagine their shocked reactions. As she parked in front of their house, she was a giant mess of nerves. Weeks ago, Sly had pointed out that she was afraid of them. Although Lana had denied it, she *was*.

Which was embarrassing for a thirty-two-year-old woman to admit, even to herself. She finally had to face those fears and move through them.

Not about to let that stop her, she squared her shoulders and entered the house.

Her parents were seated in the living room, obviously waiting for her. Mustering a smile she didn't feel, she greeted them. Her mother had set out cookies and lemonade. Having skipped dinner, Lana was famished. She ate a cookie, but was so focused on the task at hand that she barely tasted it.

"Let me guess why you're here," her mother said. "You've found a teenage girl with a baby to adopt."

"Actually, I've put the adoption idea on hold," she said. Now would be a perfect moment to announce that she was pregnant, but first things first.

Her mother looked relieved. "Is that what this visit is about? I'm glad you finally came to your senses. I was beginning to—"

"Could you save it, Mom? I need to tell you something important." Lana's mother shut her mouth. "I've met someone, a man I've fallen in love with."

Her parents shared a knowing glance. "I figured that sooner or later you would," her dad said. "But this seems a little sudden. I'd hate for you to get hurt again."

Thanks to her own actions, Lana was already suffering. "Actually, Dad, we've known each other several months."

"You kept something so momentous from your own parents?" Lana's mother shook her head. "How could you—"

"Michele," her father warned, placing a warning finger against his own lips.

"I didn't want to be judged and criticized for my choice," Lana replied.

The pained expression on her mother's face revealed that she was well aware of her own behavior. "I realize that occasionally I get on your and your sister's nerves," she said. "Surely you know that I only want the best for you."

"I get that, Mom. But I'm an adult, and I have been for a while now. It's past time that you and Dad trusted me to make my own judgments about what's best for me."

Lana's father considered that for a bit, then nodded. "I agree."

After staring at her hands, her mother raised her head. "From the moment you were born, I've guided you toward where I thought you should go. Not that you listen much anymore." Her attempt at a humorous smile failed, and she gave Lana a pleading look. "You're my daughter and it's hard to let go. But you're right, you're an adult with a good head on your shoulders."

Grateful that they understood, Lana nodded. "Thank you—both of you."

"When will your mother and I get a chance to meet this mystery man of yours?" her father asked.

"How about at dinner this Sunday?" Provided she and Sly made up and he agreed to come. Lana wouldn't let herself worry about that now.

Her parents glanced at each other again and shrugged. "That'd be nice," her father said before letting her mother take over.

"What's his name and what does he do for a living?" she asked.

Oddly calm now, and ready to test her parents' resolve to trust her, Lana sat up tall and spoke with the confidence and certainty borne out of her love for Sly. "His name is Sly Pettit. He owns Pettit Ranch."

Her mother's eyebrows jumped halfway up her forehead, and for once, she seemed at a loss for words.

Equally shocked, Lana's father opened and closed his mouth.

"Sly is a wonderful man with a good heart," Lana said. "You'll see that that when you meet him."

Her mother frowned. "I want to trust your judgment, Lana, but I'm not sure Sunday dinner is the suitable event…" At Lana's resolute expression, she broke off.

"I look forward to our weekly dinners and would hate to miss them—but if Sly isn't welcome, I won't come, either." Lana paused and bit her lip. "All I ask is that you give him a chance."

After a long, uncomfortable pause, her father cleared his throat. "If you really love him, then of course he's welcome."

Lana glanced at her mother. "Mom?"

"I won't lie to you, Lana—this upsets me." She sighed. "All right, Sly is welcome at our table. But I have no idea what your cousin will think." Her worried frown encompassed both Lana and her father.

He shook his head, then shrugged. With that, they sat back.

Lana exhaled the breath she'd been holding. "Don't worry about Cousin Tim. I'm going to drive over to his place right now and talk to him. In my heart, I'm convinced Sly didn't go near his cows."

"How can you be sure?" her mother asked.

"Because I know Sly. He'd never do that." Lana kissed both her parents. "We'll see you Sunday."

Feeling several pounds lighter, she hurried to her car.

TRAFFIC WAS LIGHT now, and Lana sped through the twilight toward the Lazy C. Convincing Cousin Tim to drop his lawsuit might be impossible, but she was determined to try. Not that she had any idea what she would say, but she'd figure it out. For the sake of her peace of mind and the future of her and Sly's unborn child, she had to.

She passed the black-and-white Pettit Ranch sign and her heart lurched painfully. She couldn't help wondering whether Sly at was home or if he'd gone out. What would he think if he knew where she was headed?

Cousin Tim's ranch was a couple hundred feet ahead. Lana signaled, slowed and pulled into the driveway. It was early evening, not quite dark yet but getting there. Yet there were no house lights on. Her cousin's truck was parked near the front door, though, which meant that he was probably at home. She pulled to a stop beside the truck and slid out of the car.

Every bit as nervous as when she'd talked to her parents, she climbed the steps and knocked at the door.

A few seconds later, Cousin Tim answered with two bottles of beer in hand. "You sure got here fas— Lana." His face was a mask of surprise. "What brings you out here?"

"Sorry, I should have called first, but I took a chance that you'd have a few minutes to talk."

Her entire adult life, she'd never stopped by to visit her cousin, but he seemed to take it in stride. "Sure, but I'm expecting someone. Come in."

He left the door cracked open, maybe for his company. A girlfriend no one was aware of? Interesting idea, but just now Lana couldn't spare a moment to speculate. She had more important things on her mind.

"Uh, you want a beer?" her cousin asked, offering her one of the bottles.

Lana shook her head. "No, thanks."

The entry opened into the living room. She still hadn't decided exactly what she was going to say, but as she crossed the worn carpet, she realized that if she spoke from the heart, she couldn't miss.

Her cousin sat down so that he was facing the door, probably to watch for his mystery guest. Lana took the armchair across from him, the one that faced the backyard. The drapes were open, and she briefly noted the fenced lawn and beyond that, rolling fields extending as far as she could see.

As soon as she settled into her seat, she got straight to the point. "I'm here to talk to you about Sly Pettit."

SLY RETURNED FROM the meeting with Haggerty in good spirits. The engineer had recently built a new home and needed help with the landscaping. He'd agreed to drastically reduce his fee for the drainage system if Sly would lay down sod and fence the front and backyards. Sly also promised to provide Haggerty with a free side of beef every year for the next ten years. The large quantity of meat would feed Haggerty's family for months.

In a few weeks, the engineer would start work on the new system. By then, Sly figured he'd be finished with the man's yard, and he and his crew could do some of the grunt work on the new drainage.

He was finishing dinner when Carpenter called. "Get your butt over here," he said. "I have some great news to share."

Anticipating a celebration, Sly had grabbed a couple of cold beers. Then, for the second time that day, he headed for the Lazy C. As he rolled up the driveway, he spotted Lana's light green sedan next to Tim's truck.

He braked to a stop. What was she doing here?

He'd bet the ranch Carpenter had no idea that he and Lana knew each other. As curious as Sly was about her reasons for being here, he was in no mood to face her. He almost turned around and left. But he was no coward. Besides, Carpenter was expecting him.

He was about to start up the front steps when he noted that the door was cracked open. In the still twilight air, Lana's voice carried easily.

Sly paused where he was, knowing he should announce his presence. But something made him keep quiet. He silently placed the beers on the second step and eavesdropped.

"Sly would never poison your cattle," she said.

What the hell? Sly frowned.

"You're friends with Pettit?" Tim asked, sounding puzzled.

"I met him before I heard about his lawsuit against you."

"You never said anything, not even when I came to your folks' for Sunday dinner last month."

"I was afraid of how they'd react, and even more scared of you. But I'm not anymore." Despite her brave words, Sly heard her swallow hard. "I just came from my parents' house, and I told them exactly what I'm telling you—that Sly and I have been seeing each other."

She'd talked to her parents? Sly could only imagine how difficult that must have been for her.

"You mean dating?" her cousin said.

"Something like that." Her voice seemed to grow stronger with each word. "You're my cousin and you're family, and that means a lot. But I can't sit by quietly and let you countersue Sly. He's a good man, an honest man. He values all cattle too much to harm them." Sly was so surprised that he had to sit down. He joined the beers on the step.

"For you to vouch for him this way, you must know him pretty well," Tim said.

"I do. Besides my dad, Sly Pettit is the best man I've ever met. I would trust him with my life."

Realizing his jaw had dropped open, Sly shut his mouth.

"That's quite a statement," Tim said.

"It's the truth. I wouldn't fall for a man I couldn't trust."

"You're in love with Sly Pettit." Carpenter sounded shocked. "Is he aware of this?"

"Not yet. I know in my very bones that he would never poison an animal. Well, maybe a mouse or a rat. I'm asking you to please drop your counter lawsuit."

"You'd side with him against me?" Gruff Tim Carpenter sounded like a hurt kid.

"I'm not siding with anyone," Lana said. "I don't believe you poisoned his cows, either. Sly would realize that, too, if you would just sit down with him and talk. Before he sued you, he tried to do that, but you wouldn't give him the time of day."

"Pettit never wanted to talk. From the get-go, he came at me with accusations."

"Then it's all the more important for the two of you to talk now. The sooner, the better. Otherwise you'll never get to the bottom of this mess."

"You're comin' at me with a damn lecture, just like Michele. Don't get me wrong, I love your mother, but her lectures give me a headache."

"I'm not my mother, and I'm not lecturing you." Lana sounded indignant. After a pause she said, "Well, darn it, maybe I am. I'll think about that later. What matters is that I'm here for a good reason. You and Sly are both hardheaded, and this lawsuit business is out of control. Someone levelheaded has to intervene. That would be me."

Him, stubborn? Sly barely stifled a loud snort.

But he had to admit that Lana was right. His head was as hard as the concrete step under him. Instead of approaching Tim Carpenter as someone who could help him find the answers he sought, Sly had accused, tried and found the man guilty.

In jumping to conclusions, he'd created a world of trouble.

Tuesday night he'd done the same thing with Lana, brushing off her suggestion that they talk. He'd been suffering mightily ever since, and guessed that she had been, too.

But even hurting, she was here, fighting for him because she loved him. She loved him.

Sly thought he might love her, too. No, he knew—he did love her.

Accepting and admitting this blew him away. He should have been scared, but wasn't. The truth was, he didn't feel half-bad—except when he realized he'd almost lost out on a lifetime with Lana.

What a damn fool he'd been.

He stood, brushed off his butt and grabbed the beers. Making no effort to be quiet, he strode up the steps. Neither Lana nor Tim was speaking, and Sly figured they'd heard his footsteps.

He knocked, then without waiting for an answer, stepped inside. The shock on Lana's face was comical, but this was no time for laughter.

"I was starting to wonder if you'd ever show up," Tim said.

"I've been here for a while now. Hold these, will you?" Sly handed him the beers, then turned to Lana. "Did you mean what you said? Do you really love me?"

"You were eavesdropping?"

Unashamed, he nodded. "I didn't expect to find you here tonight, but I spotted your car next to Tim's truck. He left the door open, and I wanted to hear what you were saying."

"You heard it all?" she asked, looking wary.

"I heard what matters—that you believe in me." Needing to touch her, Sly clasped both her hands and pulled her to her feet. "That's awesome—you're awesome."

Holding back none of his feelings, he kissed her thoroughly.

When he pulled back. Lana wore a dazed expression. "I love you, Sly."

Smiling, he gently brushed the hair out of her eyes. "Don't fall over when I say it, but I love you, too."

Tim growled. "If you two don't quit with the mushy stuff, I swear, I'll bring the hose in here and spray you down."

Sly and Lana laughed.

Not about to let go of his woman, Sly sat down in the armchair and pulled her onto his lap.

"I can't believe you're sitting in my cousin's living room," Lana said. "What are you doing here—with two beers each?"

"Sly's here because I invited him to come back," Tim said.

"Come back?" Lana echoed, confused.

Sly nodded. "I was here this afternoon, when Tim and I patched up our differences."

"Hold on a darned minute." Lana slanted her cousin a look. "You let me go through my whole spiel about how stubborn you and Sly both are without once mentioning that you'd already settled things?"

"I wanted to hear what you had to say," Tim said. "And it wasn't quite settled, but it is now."

"Will one of you please explain what's going on?" she asked.

Sly caught her up on what he knew, then turned to Tim. "I'm guessing Sheriff Dean called."

"About an hour ago. It took a while for him to find Pitch and get him to talk, but he finally confessed. It's just as I figured—he set us both up.

"I talked to my lawyer. First thing in the morning, he'll contact yours. He doubts that either of us is likely to get any restitution from Pitch. He's broke—he's always broke. But he'll probably spend a few years in jail."

"That's good enough for me," Sly said.

Carpenter nodded. "From now on, if we have issues with each other, let's talk them through."

"You have my word on that." Sly tipped up Lana's head and kissed the tip of her nose. "So do you."

"All this talk has made me thirsty." Carpenter reached for the bottle opener on the coffee table. "Have a cool one with us, Lana? There's a glass in the kitchen."

"Um, I can't." She looked at Sly. "We should tell him."

"Before your sister or your parents or Dani?"

She nodded. "After watching us get all mushy, it's the least we can do. Okay with you?" When Sly nodded, she glanced at her cousin. "Do me a favor, and don't contact the family for another forty-eight hours."

Carpenter seemed surprised by the request, but shrugged. "I guess I can do that. What's this about?"

Before making their announcement, Sly and Lana stood up. She threaded her fingers with his, and he nodded at her to do the talking.

"Sly and I... We're expecting a baby."

Her cousin almost choked on his beer. "Say what?"

Sly nodded. "It's true. The due date is early January."

"That's not long to wait," Carpenter said. "Congratulations, you two. It's a damn good thing we settled this cattle business."

He shook hands with Sly and patted Lana's shoulder. "I know how difficult your parents can be, Lana," he said. "If you want me to be there when you give them the news, I'll vouch for Sly."

"You'd do that?" Lana smiled at him. "Has anyone ever told you that you're a nice guy?" Standing on her toes, she kissed her cousin's cheek. Even his ears turned red. "Your offer means a lot, but Sly and I will do it together."

Chapter Twenty

"I haven't been to the falls in ages," Lana commented as Sly drove down River Drive early Saturday morning. "This will be fun—even if you did wake me up at the crack of dawn on my day to sleep in."

Remembering exactly how that had gone down, Sly gave her a heavy-lidded look. "You didn't seem to mind."

"Only because waking up to your kisses is a lot more fun than an alarm clock." Wearing the glow of a woman thoroughly loved, she smiled.

Sly grinned at her. Neither of them had slept much last night. They'd been too busy making love and talking. In the wee hours, Sly had come up with the plan for a picnic breakfast at the falls, followed by visits to Lana's sister and Dani.

He was happier than he'd been since… He couldn't recall ever feeling this fantastic. He enjoyed having Lana in his bed and didn't think he'd ever grow tired of waking up beside her.

The very idea would have terrified him a few months ago. Today he felt like the luckiest man alive.

They headed into Prosperity Park, where woods and acres of manicured lawn surrounded the falls. "There's the gift shop where Kate works," Lana said. "Too bad it's so early. Otherwise we could stop in and visit her."

Sly wanted Lana all to himself for a couple of hours, which was why he'd suggested the early-morning picnic. "We'll catch her another time."

"Who should we tell first—my sister or yours?" Lana asked as Sly drove past walking and hiking trails, toward the falls.

"You remember how swamped Big Mama's is on Saturday mornings, especially during tourist season. Let's talk to your sister first, then drive over to the restaurant and grab Dani for a quick break. Why don't we finish up by stopping in at your parents'? I'd hate to spring the baby on them during my first Sunday dinner."

A week ago, the suggestion would have upset or worried her. Today, she looked calm and assured. "This afternoon it is." She glanced at the clock on the dash. "It's seven-thirty, and Liz is sure to be up. I'm going to call and make sure she'll be home later."

By the time Lana finished the call to her sister, Sly had parked in the large lot near the falls. Picnic basket and blanket in hand, they took the pathway that led to the falls, sauntering past beautiful flower gardens. As Sly had intended, at this early hour they had the place to themselves. Birds twittered in the trees, and playful squirrels chattered and chased each other. In the distance he heard the unmistakable sound of a waterfall.

A quarter mile later, the path curved sharply south, revealing a stunning view of the falls.

The sight of the steep rocks jutting several dozen yards up from the earth and the powerful cascade of water spilling over them in a thick curtain of spray never ceased to amaze Sly. He and Lana both stopped to take in the sight.

"This view always takes my breath away." Lana's chin tipped up and wonder filled her face. "How beautiful they are."

As Sly gazed down at her, warmth and tenderness

flooded his chest, and he silently swore to do everything in his power to make Lana happy. "You're the beautiful one," he said. Then he kissed her.

Because they were in public, he kept it shorter and lighter than he would have preferred. Regardless, she was flushed and breathless when he pulled away.

His passionate woman.

The love in her eyes humbled him, and he was sure that life didn't get much better than this.

A safe distance from the reach of the water's spray, they found a flat, grassy place perfect for a picnic. Sly spread out the blanket, and Lana helped set out the food Mrs. Rutland had prepared for his weekend alone. Sly planned to introduce his woman to his housekeeper in the very near future. Mrs. R was going to like Lana. His crew, too.

Despite enjoying a snack in the middle of the night, the long night of lovemaking had made them both ravenous. For a while they forgot about conversation and chowed down. Lana's hearty appetite was one more thing Sly loved about her.

"Do you think your parents will be upset about the baby?" he asked, smiling to himself as she filched a chunk of his blueberry muffin.

"I won't lie—I want them to be happy about it. If they're not, I'll be sad," she said. "But I love you and you love me, and no matter what they think or say, that's the bottom line."

Sly couldn't have dreamed up a better reply. He felt as if he'd waited all his life for the amazing woman sharing his blanket.

So what are you waiting for? a voice whispered in his head.

In that moment, he made up his mind. He pushed the plates aside and knelt on the blanket, pulling Lana up to face him. She gave him a questioning look.

"I don't have a ring or anything, but I'd be…" Suddenly choked up, he stopped to clear his throat. "Lana, I want… Oh, hell." He was going to lose it.

"If this is a proposal, the answer is yes!"

"No kidding?"

"I've never been more serious in my life."

She wrapped her arms around his neck and he kissed her again, with all the love in his heart. When they came up for air, she rested her forehead against his and sighed. "I now have exactly what I've always dreamed of." She moved away from him and sat down again. "There's only one problem."

Unable to think what it could be, Sly gave a puzzled frown and tilted up her chin. "We solved all our problems. Tim and I dropped our lawsuits, we're about to tell your parents about the baby and we're getting married."

"I'm talking about the beautiful mural I painted in the nursery. What am I supposed to do with the town house?"

"Sell it or keep it as a rental—whatever you decide is okay by me. Heck, if you want, paint murals in all the bedrooms at my place."

"Your house is definitely big enough for a family."

"A whole houseful of kids, if I have my way." Picturing several little Lanas running around, creating pandemonium, he grinned.

"What if this is our only pregnancy?" she asked, suddenly somber.

"Then we'll adopt. Either way, I consider myself the luckiest man in the world."

The love and trust shining from Lana's eyes filled Sly with sweet certainty that no matter where life took him, Lana would be at his side.

"Come on." He rose to his feet and pulled her up beside him. "Let's go share our good news."

Two years later

"YOU'RE AWFULLY QUIET this afternoon," Sly said as he parked in front of Lana's parents' house for Sunday dinner. "Feeling okay?"

Being a rancher's wife and the mother of a toddler, not to mention setting up the second day care and finding a capable person to manage it, made for some very busy times, but Lana wouldn't have traded her life for anything. "I could use a nap, thanks to a certain little someone waking me up in the middle of the night."

She turned around to smile at their beautiful daughter, Johanna, named after Sly's mother.

The little girl beamed, her straight blond hair flying as she bounced in her seat. "'Hanna see cousins and Gammy and Gampa."

"That's right, sweetie," Lana said.

"She's already talking in full sentences, and she's barely eighteen months old," he said proudly.

"Smart like her daddy."

"And her mom."

Lana and Sly grinned at each other. She leaned toward her husband for a quick kiss. "Have I told you lately that I adore you, Mr. Pettit?"

"Not since early this morning, when you and I, uh—" He glanced at their daughter in the rearview mirror. "When we were in bed."

Lana was lost in his eyes when Johanna let out an excited shriek. "Cousins!"

Liz and Eric had just arrived, and Connor and Emma were racing toward the car.

Johanna wanted out. Sly lifted her from her car seat in time for her to cousins to greet her. Moments later, Connor and Emma raced for the backyard, Johanna squealing and toddling after them.

Eric nodded at Sly. "Come on, let's catch up to our kids."

"What you guys really want is the chance to check out Dad's new grill," Liz teased with a wry smile.

Neither man denied it.

Lana and her sister followed behind, catching each other up on the busy week they'd both had.

In the yard, Lana's parents greeted everyone with smiles and hugs. Lana's mother smiled at Sly. "Guess what I found at the specialty store? That microbrew beer you've been wanting to try."

"Thanks, Michele." Sly kissed her cheek. "You're the best."

After two years, Lana still marveled at the warm relationship her mother shared with Sly—better than she would ever have imagined.

Her dad clapped his hands on Sly's and Eric's shoulders and steered them toward the smoking grill, where steaks were sizzling. "Wait'll I show you what this baby can do."

Some fifteen minutes later, as everyone headed for the picnic table, Lana's father gave his head an admiring shake. "What a beautiful family we have."

Lana couldn't have agreed more.

* * * * *

REQUEST YOUR FREE BOOKS!
2 FREE NOVELS PLUS 2 FREE GIFTS!

H HARLEQUIN®

American ★ Romance®

LOVE, HOME & HAPPINESS

YES! Please send me 2 FREE Harlequin® American Romance® novels and my 2 FREE gifts (gifts are worth about $10). After receiving them, if I don't wish to receive any more books, I can return the shipping statement marked "cancel." If I don't cancel, I will receive 4 brand-new novels every month and be billed just $4.74 per book in the U.S. or $5.24 per book in Canada. That's a savings of at least 14% off the cover price! It's quite a bargain! Shipping and handling is just 50¢ per book in the U.S. and 75¢ per book in Canada.* I understand that accepting the 2 free books and gifts places me under no obligation to buy anything. I can always return a shipment and cancel at any time. Even if I never buy another book, the two free books and gifts are mine to keep forever.

154/354 HDN F4YN

Name _____ (PLEASE PRINT) _____

Address _____ Apt. #_____

City _____ State/Prov. _____ Zip/Postal Code _____

Signature (if under 18, a parent or guardian must sign) _____

Mail to the Harlequin® Reader Service:
IN U.S.A.: P.O. Box 1867, Buffalo, NY 14240-1867
IN CANADA: P.O. Box 609, Fort Erie, Ontario L2A 5X3

Want to try two free books from another line?
Call 1-800-873-8635 or visit www.ReaderService.com.

* Terms and prices subject to change without notice. Prices do not include applicable taxes. Sales tax applicable in N.Y. Canadian residents will be charged applicable taxes. Offer not valid in Quebec. This offer is limited to one order per household. Not valid for current subscribers to Harlequin American Romance books. All orders subject to credit approval. Credit or debit balances in a customer's account(s) may be offset by any other outstanding balance owed by or to the customer. Please allow 4 to 6 weeks for delivery. Offer available while quantities last.

Your Privacy—The Harlequin® Reader Service is committed to protecting your privacy. Our Privacy Policy is available online at www.ReaderService.com or upon request from the Harlequin Reader Service.

We make a portion of our mailing list available to reputable third parties that offer products we believe may interest you. If you prefer that we not exchange your name with third parties, or if you wish to clarify or modify your communication preferences, please visit us at www.ReaderService.com/consumerchoice or write to us at Harlequin Reader Service Preference Service, P.O. Box 9062, Buffalo, NY 14269. Include your complete name and address.

HARI3R

SPECIAL EXCERPT FROM

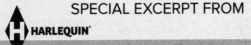

*Welcome to **BRIDESMAIDS CREEK**,*
Tina Leonard's new miniseries featuring wild, hunky
cowboys and adorable babies.

Read on for an excerpt from
THE REBEL COWBOY'S QUADRUPLETS
by New York Times *bestselling author Tina Leonard.*

"Can I help you?"

"I'm looking for Mackenzie Hawthorne. My name's Justin Morant."

"I'm Mackenzie."

Pink lips smiled at him, brown eyes sparkled, and he drew back a little, astonished by how darling she was smiling at him like that. Like he was some kind of hero who'd just rolled up on his white steed.

And damn, he was driving a white truck.

Which was kind of funny, if you appreciated irony, and right now, he felt like he was living it.

Sudden baby wails caught his attention, and hers, too.

"Come on in," she said. "You'll have to excuse me for just a moment. But make yourself at home in the kitchen. There's tea on the counter, and Mrs. Harper's put together a lovely chicken salad. After I feed the babies, we can talk about what kind of work you're looking for."

The tiny brunette disappeared, allowing him a better look at blue jeans that accentuated her curves.

Damn Ty for pulling this prank on him. His buddy was probably laughing his fool ass off right about now, knowing how Justin felt about settling down and family ties in general. Justin was a loner, at least in spirit. He had lots of

HAREXPO714

friends on the circuit, and he was from a huge family. He had three brothers, all as independent as he was, except for J.T., who liked to stay close to the family and the neighborhood he'd grown up in.

Justin was going to continue to ride alone.

Mrs. Harper smiled at him as he took a barstool at the wide kitchen island. "Welcome, Justin."

"Thank you," he replied, not about to let himself feel welcome. He needed to get out of here as fast as possible. This place was a honey trap of food and good intentions.

He needed a job, but not this job. And the last thing he wanted to do was work for a woman with soft doe eyes and a place that was teetering on becoming unmanageable. From the little he'd seen, there was a lot to do. He had a bum knee and a bad feeling about this, and no desire to be around children.

On the other hand, it couldn't hurt to help out for a week, maybe two, tops. Could it?

Look for THE REBEL COWBOY'S QUADRUPLETS,
*the first story in the **BRIDESMAIDS CREEK** miniseries*
by USA TODAY bestselling author Tina Leonard, from
Harlequin® American Romance®.
Available July 2014, wherever books and ebooks are sold.

HAREXP0714

HARLEQUIN®

American Romance®

She wasn't looking for love

Savannah Baron is determined to turn The Peach Pit from a simple roadside stand on her family's Texas ranch into a bustling country store. She's too busy with her business to even enter many rodeos anymore, let alone date. But when a health scare prompts her to search for her long-estranged mother, she discovers more than a helping hand in an old friend.

Soldier-turned-private-investigator Travis Shepard never thought he'd move on after his wife's tragic death, yet with Savannah, the walls he built around his heart begin to crumble away. He admires her quiet strength and beauty. But Savannah still faces a medical crisis, and Travis can't bear the idea of losing anyone else. Can he find the strength to love again?

Look for
The Texan's Cowgirl Bride
by TRISH MILBURN
from the *Texas Rodeo Barons* miniseries.

Available July 2014 from Harlequin® American Romance® wherever books and ebooks are sold.

Also available from the *Texas Rodeo Barons* miniseries:
THE TEXAN'S BABY
by *New York Times* bestselling author Donna Alward

www.Harlequin.com